MAGNUM TE...

THE EVERLASTING NIGHTMARE

Foreword

Dear Readers,

Welcome to the shadowed realms where reality and nightmare intertwine, and the echoes of eldritch symphonies resonate through the corridors of the unknown. I am Magnum Tenebrosum, your guide through the veiled horror and cosmic revelation tapestries.

As you embark on this literary journey, know that you tread upon the precipice of the extraordinary. The tales woven within these pages are not mere narratives but portals to realms where the boundaries of the imaginable are stretched, and the fabric of reality is woven with threads of eldritch chaos.

In the depths of Lovecraftian Cosmic Horror, where the ordinary meets the extraordinary, you will encounter protagonists facing the unfathomable, confronting gods that dream unsettling dreams and witnessing landscapes morphing into surreal nightmares. The eldritch symphony, a celestial harmony that transcends mortal comprehension, will guide you through cosmic confrontations and chaotic dances that bridge the realms of Fantasia and the waking world.

As you turn the quiescent pages, remember that you are not a passive observer but an active participant in a transcendental experience. The characters within may face nightmarish embodiments, struggle against intensifying discord, and confront the very essence of cosmic upheaval. Yet, amid the chaos, they find resilience and symbiotic connections that echo in the hushed corridors of Fantasia.

"The Everlasting Nightmare" is not just a collection of stories; it is an exploration of the ineffable, an odyssey into the depths of the human psyche when confronted with the cosmic unknown. Aria and Daniel, forever changed by the eldritch saga, invite you to traverse the cosmic tapestry with them, to reflect on the cosmic mirror that shapes destinies, and to embrace the endless horizons that follow the echoes of silence.

May these tales leave an indelible mark on your imagination, and may the eldritch symphony's resonance linger in the quiescent spaces between the words. Brace yourselves, dear readers, for the shadows are alive, and the everlasting nightmare awaits within them.

Yours in the cosmic unknown,

Magnum Tenebrosum

Prologue
The Occult Enclave

I stood before the weathered door, its surface etched with cryptic symbols that seemed to shimmer in the dim light of flickering candles. The air carried the musty scent of forgotten knowledge, a scent that clung to the very fabric of the ancient texts within. My name is Aria Evernight, and I am a wanderer searching for the esoteric, drawn to the mysteries that whispered through the veil of reality.

As the door creaked open, revealing the occult bookstore's dimly lit interior, I immersed myself in a realm of arcane wonders. The shelves, sagging under the weight of ancient tomes, stretched into the shadows, their contents whispering secrets to those willing to listen. Each step resonated with the echoes of countless seekers who had treaded the creaking wooden floor before me.

The atmosphere was suffused with a mysterious ambiance that seemed to dance with the flickering candles, casting shadows that played hide-and-seek among the forgotten knowledge. It was a sanctuary for the seekers of the unknown, an enclave where the boundaries between the mundane and the arcane blurred.

In the hushed corners, I discovered myriad texts adorned with symbols that defied conventional understanding. The words within held the promise of forbidden truths, and I, Aria Evernight, was here to uncover the mysteries that lay dormant within the ancient pages.

Another protagonist, Daniel Eldrith, embarked on his journey into the occult on the other side of the dim-lit enclave.

I pushed open the heavy door, its aged wood groaning in protest as I entered the esoteric bookstore. I am Daniel Eldrith, a seeker of the unknown, compelled by an insatiable curiosity that often led me to places shrouded in mystique.

The setting within was unlike anything I had encountered before. The dimly lit interior seemed to breathe with the weight of centuries, the shelves adorned with tomes that whispered tales of forgotten realms. The musty aroma of ancient knowledge filled the air, mingling with the scent of candle wax.

As I wandered through the labyrinthine shelves, the flickering candles cast dancing shadows, creating an almost alive atmosphere. Arcane symbols adorned the shelves and walls, adding to the enigmatic aura that permeated the space. I couldn't help but be drawn to the mysterious corners where hidden knowledge awaited discovery.

The descriptions of the occult bookstore's interior played tricks on my senses, the essence of the place resonating with a sense of history that went beyond the physicality of the books. It was as if the ancient tomes held a collective memory, waiting for someone like me to unlock their secrets.

In this enclave of esoteric wisdom, Aria and I, two seekers with intertwined destinies, embarked on a journey that would lead us beyond the boundaries of ordinary understanding. The dim-lit sanctuary held the promise of revelations, and little did we know that our paths were about to converge in ways that defied the limitations of mortal perception.

In the bustling city where history and mystery intertwined, Daniel Eldrith, a budding historian with an insatiable curiosity, navigated the crowded streets with purpose. His footsteps, guided by the whispers of ancient tales, echoed through the urban labyrinth.

Daniel, with his ever-present notebook and a backpack slung over one shoulder, was a figure of perpetual exploration. He sought the untold stories, the enigmatic fragments that lay beneath the surface of accepted narratives. The dusty shelves of libraries and forgotten corners of museums were his sanctuaries.

His character, that of an inquisitive historian, manifested in how he absorbed every detail of the past. His fingers traced the worn spines of ancient tomes, and his eyes gleamed excitedly at the prospect of uncharted historical anomalies. He was a seeker, driven by an insatiable hunger for knowledge that propelled him into the obscure recesses of history.

As legends circulated through the city, tales of eldritch disturbances, mysterious cults, and cosmic anomalies became the focal point of Daniel's fascination. The air crackled with the energy of whispered secrets, and the stories took on their own life. His pursuit of understanding became a relentless quest, and the city became a canvas for the unfolding mysteries.

Daniel's figure stood out among the bustling crowds—an inquisitive historian on the verge of unlocking the secrets that lingered in the shadows. The legends that danced through the air became threads woven into the fabric of his journey. Each step propelled him deeper into the heart of the unknown, where the past and the present converged in a tapestry of enigma.

The city, with its hidden tales and unspoken truths, awaited the inquisitive historian's next revelation. Daniel Eldrith's quest for understanding would soon transcend the limits of conventional knowledge, propelling him into a journey that promised to unravel the mysteries woven into the very fabric of the urban landscape.

In the quiet enclave of the occult bookstore, Daniel Eldrith, the inquisitive historian, found himself drawn to a particular volume that seemed to pulse with hidden energy—"The Everlasting Nightmare." It lay nestled among other esoteric tomes, its cover adorned with cryptic symbols that whispered promises of arcane knowledge.

As his fingers traced the spine, a subtle pull compelled him to liberate the enigmatic tome from its resting place. The weight of the book in his hands hinted at the significance held within its pages. Daniel couldn't resist the call of its mysterious contents.

Daniel embarked on a journey into the cosmic narrative hidden within its pages with the enigmatic book in hand. As he opened the cover, the intricate lines and symbols revealed themselves, challenging his initial perception of a mere grimoire. The unfolding tale transcended ordinary incantations, drawing him into the cosmic dance of eldritch forces.

Each turned page formed an inexplicable connection between Daniel and the unfolding narrative. The cosmic events described within seemed to echo the legends whispered in the city's corners, and with each passing moment, the boundaries between his reality and the cosmic events blurred. A symbiosis emerged, entwining Daniel's consciousness with the eldritch tale woven into "The Everlasting Nightmare." The pages became a gateway, leading him into a surreal landscape where reality and cosmic lore converged, setting the stage for a fateful journey beyond the veil of ordinary understanding.

Part I
The Eclipsing Dreams

Chapter 1
Whispers in the Shadows

In the heart of the city's hustle and bustle, where the resonance of history echoed through its cobblestone arteries, Daniel Eldrith carved a niche as an unwavering investigator propelled by an insatiable curiosity. His journey unfolded as a relentless pursuit, weaving through the labyrinth of enigmas that interconnected the threads of bygone eras and the contemporary world.

As the inquisitive historian, Daniel's portrait depicted a man immersed in the pursuit of forgotten tales and unsolved riddles and the exploration of the esoteric. Dusty archives and forgotten tomes were the realms where he sought solace. Still, beyond the conventional narratives, his yearning extended to the enigmatic, to the mysteries that defied the constraints of logical explanations.

The city's whispers, like ethereal messengers, found their way to Daniel's attentive ears, carried by the wind through narrow alleyways and concealed corners. These murmurs spoke of eldritch phenomena, mysterious cults weaving clandestine rituals, and cosmic anomalies that teased the boundaries of comprehension. Each rumor became an invitation, a siren's call pulling Daniel into uncharted territories where every shadow held the promise of an untold story.

Navigating the urban landscape, Daniel saw the allure of the unknown, painting the city as a vast canvas with tales waiting to be unraveled. The whispers in the shadows transformed into a captivating melody, a rhythmic dance with the esoteric that lured him further into the depths of the unknown. However, unbeknownst to him, these whispers were not merely fragments of tales but threads intricately woven into a larger narrative that transcended the ordinary.

With its hidden tales and unspoken truths, the city stood as a grand stage for Daniel Eldrith's exploration. Each step he took into the enigmatic corners of the urban sprawl propelled him deeper into a story that tested the limits of his understanding, promising to unveil mysteries that had lain dormant in the shadows for far too long. Little did he fathom the cosmic dance that awaited, where the dreams of the waking world would be eclipsed by eldritch nightmares concealed in the secret folds of reality.

In the tapestry of the city's secrets, my journey into the unknown deepened, becoming an intricate dance with the eldritch. The whispers of esoteric occurrences resonated through hidden alleys and forgotten corners, drawing me into a world where the boundaries of reality blurred and the arcane took center stage.

Day by day, I ventured into the unexplored realms within the city, where mysteries lay hidden like ghosts awaiting acknowledgment. Peculiar happenings became guideposts, each enigma an invitation to delve deeper into the hidden facets of the urban sprawl. The enigmatic city unfolded its layers, revealing cryptic symbols and arcane energies that fueled my insatiable curiosity.

One such instance etched itself into my consciousness—a weathered symbol painted on a wall, its significance lost in time. Yet, the air around it vibrated with otherworldly energy, as if the very fabric of reality quivered in its presence. It became a puzzle, a riddle challenging my understanding, igniting a fervor to decode the cryptic language of the eldritch that whispered through the city's veins.

The old library transformed into a haven of shadows and secrets as night descended. The air within its abandoned halls hummed with the whispers of forgotten tales. I found myself drawn to a book whose pages exuded an ethereal aura. Each word seemed to resonate with a cosmic energy, a prelude to the grand narrative that awaited me—a narrative woven with dreams, nightmares, and the intricate threads binding them together.

These initial probes, seemingly disparate, were threads woven into the fabric of my growing prowess in eldritch investigations. With its concealed whispers and cryptic symbols, the city became a vast canvas upon which I painted the story of my relentless pursuit of the unknown. Each discovery expanded my comprehension of the eldritch and revealed a profound awareness—the city held secrets that transcended the understanding of ordinary eyes. As the seeker, I was merely scratching its arcane tapestry's surface.

The city's pulse quickened with rumors, a melodic hum echoing through the crowded streets and quiet corners. Like elusive specters, whispers spoke of enigmatic cults and their purported entanglement in eldritch disturbances. Locals traded tales of cosmic anomalies, their voices a blend of awe and trepidation, as if the very air bore witness to secrets hidden in the city's heart.

Among these tales, a subtle thread connected the enigmatic cults to my quest for knowledge. Rumors painted a canvas of eldritch disturbances, each stroke revealing the intricate dance between the unknown and the known. The whispers became a symphony, and the cosmic disturbances resonated with a growing intensity with each note.

As I delved into the esoteric annals of the city, the whispers became my guide, leading me to places where the mundane met the eldritch. The stories of cults and cosmic upheavals intertwined, forming a narrative transcending reality's boundaries. It was like the city was an oracle, revealing its secrets to those who dared to listen.

In the shadowed corners of Fantasia, where the Dreamlands intertwined with the cosmic whispers of the waking world, Aria Evernight felt the subtle tremors of disturbances echoing through the fabric of her reality. Whispers of enigmatic cults reached even the realms of dreams, painting the landscapes with hues of uncertainty.

The cosmic disturbances manifested in the Dreamlands are unsettling ripples, disturbing the tranquility of Fantasia. Eldritch entities, the weavers of dreams, sensed the subtle shifts in the cosmic symphony. Aria, attuned to the eldritch rhythms, felt the threads of her reality intertwining with the echoes of the waking world.

The connection, though tenuous, drew her closer to the enigma that unfolded. In the interplay of dreams and reality, Aria sensed a presence. This force mirrored the eldritch disturbances in the waking world. It was as if the cosmic ballet orchestrated by unseen hands in the city's alleys had cast its echoes into Fantasia, disturbing the once prevailed harmonious balance.

The whispers of cosmic disturbances wove together the fates of Daniel and Aria, binding their stories in a cosmic tapestry that unfolded across realms. The eldritch disturbances, a bridge between their worlds, became the guiding melody leading them further into the heart of a narrative that transcended the boundaries of waking and dreaming realities.

—

With its labyrinthine streets and concealed alleys, the city harbored shadows—ephemeral entities that danced at the edges of perception. Mysterious figures, cloaked in the veil of the unknown, lurked in the corners where light struggled to penetrate. Within these shadows, the enigma of the eldritch disturbances began to take tangible form.

As I navigated the city's underbelly, these unseen shadows became palpable. Their existence was not merely whispered folklore but a living, breathing reality that resonated with each step I took. The air seemed to ripple with energy transcending the material, and the shadows whispered secrets that eluded the grasp of mundane understanding.

The mysterious figures, mere silhouettes in the periphery, hinted at a deeper, darker narrative—one intertwined with the cosmic disturbances that had become the focal point of my investigations. Like spectral guides, the shadows beckoned me further into the labyrinth, urging me to uncover the truths obscured by the veils of the eldritch.

—

In Fantasia, where shadows played with the ethereal glow of eldritch energies, Aria Evernight sensed the subtle disturbances that echoed through the Dreamlands. Shadows of the unseen, entities born of cosmic whispers, moved in tandem with the eldritch disturbances. Their forms were fluid, weaving through the tapestry of dreams with an otherworldly grace.

Aria's awareness expanded beyond the tangible landscapes of Fantasia, reaching into the shadows that hinted at the unseen forces at play. Eldritch entities, veiled in the obscurity of dreams, manifested as shifting shadows that mirrored the mysterious figures in the waking world. The threads of connection between these shadows and the disturbances in the city's reality became more pronounced.

Aria's perception of the unseen deepened as the cosmic symphony played its haunting melody. The shadows in Fantasia and the waking world intertwined in a dance that blurred the boundaries of perception and reality. The realization dawned that these shadows were not mere specters but integral threads in the cosmic tapestry—a tapestry that Daniel and Aria were destined to unravel.

The shadows of the unseen, both in the city's streets and the dreamscapes of Fantasia, became conduits to a deeper understanding. Daniel's growing awareness mirrored Aria's realization that the eldritch disturbances were not isolated incidents but threads woven by unseen hands, connecting their destinies in ways they were yet to comprehend.

Chapter 2
The Occult Bookstore

The city's rhythmic heartbeat, a subtle cadence beneath the hustle of everyday life, led Daniel Eldrith to an unassuming corner, a sanctuary of the arcane hidden within the urban sprawl. The occult bookstore, a relic of forgotten wisdom, emerged like a spectral mirage. Its exterior, marked by the passage of time, stood as a testament to the secrets held within its walls.

Approaching the enigmatic entrance felt like stepping into a forgotten realm. The bricks, weathered by countless seasons, bore the silent tales of past eras. Symbols, etched with an otherworldly precision, adorned the facade, beckoning those attuned to their language. The wrought-iron sign, hanging delicately as if in silent contemplation, creaked with the secrets it held.

As Daniel stood before the threshold, the air shimmered with arcane energy, and the entrance exuded a magnetic pull. The atmosphere seemed charged with anticipation, promising the unveiling of mysteries yet unraveled. The door, a guardian between worlds, yielded with a reluctant grace as Daniel crossed into the store's embrace.

The exterior, cloaked in the perpetual twilight of the city's shadows, wore the scars of narratives etched into its brick canvas. The wrought-iron sign swayed gently, a sentinel greeting those who dared venture into its depths. Beyond the heavy drapes, the windows revealed a glimpse of ancient tomes resting on timeworn shelves. Flickering candles glow warmly, their dance accentuating the arcane symbols etched into the glass.

The faded name on the storefront, almost whispering forgotten truths, hinted at the wealth of knowledge concealed within. The air surrounding the entrance vibrated with a spectral hum as if the store acknowledged the seekers drawn to its mysteries.

With each step across the threshold, the magnetic resonance intensified. Though worn by the passage of countless hands, the door seemed to acknowledge Daniel's presence with a quiet acknowledgment. The interior, saturated with the scent of aged paper and the musty aroma of ancient secrets, enveloped him in a sensory symphony.

The subtle pull became a tangible force, guiding Daniel through the labyrinth of shelves, each laden with volumes whispering tales of forgotten realms. Like a living entity, the bookstore seemed attuned to his quest for knowledge, and the boundaries between the ordinary and the mystical blurred with every passing moment. The subtle pull hinted at the store's contents and a destiny entwined with the fabric of eldritch disturbances lurking in the city's shadows.

While Daniel delved into the mysteries of the bookstore in Fantasia, Aria Evernight felt the ripples of his journey through the cosmic currents. The eldritch disturbances mirrored in the Dreamlands, where shadows danced with an ethereal glow, hinting at a connection yet unveiled.

As Daniel stepped into the occult enclave, the shadows in Fantasia stirred, resonating with the subtle shifts in the cosmic energies. Aria, a spectral observer within her dreamlike domain, felt the reverberations of Daniel's footsteps as if they echoed through the fabric of Fantasia. The eldritch entities, veiled in the obscurity of dreams, became aware of the awakening cosmic symphony.

In the waking world, Daniel's investigations extended beyond the occult bookstore. Whispers among locals hinted at enigmatic cults with alleged ties to the city's eldritch disturbances. As Daniel traversed the urban landscape, the rumors became a breadcrumb trail, guiding him deeper into the labyrinth of hidden knowledge.

The tales spoke of clandestine gatherings, symbols etched in hidden places, and a cosmic dance that transcended mortal understanding. The occult bookstore, a focal point in this cosmic ballet, became a nexus where the whispers of the city and the eldritch disturbances intertwined.

Within Fantasia, where shadows played with the ethereal glow of eldritch energies, Aria sensed the subtle disturbances that echoed through the Dreamlands. Shadows of the unseen, entities born of cosmic whispers, moved in tandem with the eldritch disturbances. Their forms were fluid, weaving through the tapestry of dreams with an otherworldly grace.

Aria's awareness expanded beyond the tangible landscapes of Fantasia, reaching into the shadows that hinted at the unseen forces at play. Eldritch entities, veiled in the obscurity of dreams, manifested as shifting shadows that watched and waited. The cosmic dance mirrored the waking world's rumors, drawing Aria's attention to the convergence of the realities ahead.

The cosmic threads, connecting Daniel's exploration of the occult enclave and Aria's spectral observation in Fantasia, hinted at a symbiotic dance between the waking world and the Dreamlands. As Daniel continued his journey through the occult bookstore, the cosmic symphony resonated, laying the foundation for an intertwining narrative that transcended the boundaries of mortal understanding.

As I ventured deeper into the occult enclave, the transition from daylight to the dimly lit interior was almost imperceptible. Shadows clung to the shelves like ancient guardians, and the air seemed to resonate with the weight of forgotten knowledge. Dim lighting cast elongated shadows over the narrow aisles, each step echoing through the quiet sanctum.

The shelves, sagging under the weight of centuries-old tomes, whispered tales of past epochs. Leather-bound volumes, their covers embossed with symbols that hinted at arcane wisdom, stood like sentinels along the narrow passages. Flickering candles, strategically placed to accentuate the mystique, added an ethereal glow to the dimly lit aisles.

Within this cocoon of shadows and soft illumination, the musty scent of aged parchment intertwined with the occasional aroma of ancient herbs. It was a sensory journey through time and forbidden knowledge, where each step felt like trespassing on the threshold of secrets guarded by unseen forces.

The atmosphere hummed with anticipation as if the walls absorbed the whispers of eldritch truths. I moved with reverence, aware that every volume housed words and echoes of cosmic forces waiting to be unraveled. The bookstore was a silent oracle, its secrets veiled in the play of light and shadow, inviting me to partake in its enigmatic revelations.

In Fantasia, as I navigated the dimly lit aisles of the occult bookstore, Aria Evernight sensed the echoes of my footsteps. The shadows in Fantasia, reflections of those cast by flickering candles in the waking world, danced with a cosmic rhythm. A symbiotic connection unfolded, binding the realms in a dance of light and darkness.

In Fantasia, where the boundaries between reality and dream blurred, the shadows responded to my presence. Eldritch entities, attuned to the cosmic symphony, stirred within the Dreamlands' tapestry. The dimly lit aisles of the occult bookstore became a mirrored realm in Fantasia, shadows mimicking the dance of the waking world.

The symbiotic dance between the waking world and Fantasia intensified. The subtle play of light and shadow, a reflection of the occult enclave's ambiance, echoed through the Dreamlands. As a spectral observer, Aria felt the resonance as the realms synchronized in a cosmic ballet. The eldritch forces, veiled in shadows, acknowledged the unfolding narrative, amplifying the symbiosis between my journey in the occult bookstore and the ethereal dance in Fantasia.

As the dimly lit aisles embraced both realms, the symbiotic shadows whispered secrets that transcended mortal understanding. The cosmic symphony, composed of shadows and light, painted an intricate tapestry that connected the waking world and the Dreamlands in a dance that defied the boundaries of reality.

In Fantasia, where reality twisted and contorted like a living tapestry, Aria Evernight observed the interplay of shadows that mirrored the occult enclave. The dimly lit aisles beckoned with an otherworldly allure, each step in the waking world echoing through the Dreamlands as a haunting melody.

Though existing in the waking world, the bookstore manifested within Fantasia as a surreal landscape of shifting shadows and ethereal echoes. Aria, a spectral observer, marveled at the convergence of realms, where the tangible and the intangible wove together seamlessly.

As Daniel moved through the aisles, Aria perceived an accompanying symphony. This haunting melody resonated with the cosmic forces hidden within the tomes. Each flicker of a candle in the waking world produced ripples in Fantasia, creating an ephemeral symphony that guided Aria's spectral senses through the metaphysical corridors of the Dreamlands.

—

In the dimly lit aisles, my fingertips brushed the spines of ancient volumes, feeling the pulse of eldritch energies that transcended the boundaries of the mundane. Unbeknownst to me, these subtle actions echoed in Fantasia, where Aria perceived the vibrations of my exploration.

In the waking world, I traced my fingers along the spines of tomes, their ancient textures resonating with a hidden energy. These motions reverberated through Fantasia, unseen by mortal eyes, creating ripples that whispered secrets to Aria. The symbiotic connection between us deepened as the tactile sensations in the waking world translated into ethereal echoes within the Dreamlands.

In her spectral form, Aria sensed the eldritch forces responding to my presence. Shadows, animated by cosmic energies, whispered cryptic messages transcending language boundaries. The occult enclave became a bridge between realms, where the tactile exploration of forbidden knowledge became a dance that intertwined both our fates.

As shadows and echoes harmonized, the occult bookstore emerged as a nexus of cosmic convergence in the dimly lit aisles. Unseen forces guided our steps, orchestrating a symphony that unfolded not only in the waking world but resonated through the Dreamlands, binding Aria's ethereal essence with my mortal journey. The dimly lit aisles were not just physical boundaries but thresholds into a cosmic narrative where the tangible and the intangible danced in eternal unity.

Like passages through time, the dimly lit aisles unfolded a labyrinth of esoteric knowledge. As I delved deeper into the occult bookstore, the shelves revealed their secrets, unveiling hidden tomes that pulsated with forgotten wisdom.

The shelves seemed to stretch into infinity, each book a gateway to untold mysteries. My fingers brushed against spines, seeking the resonance of ancient truths. With every step, the air thickened with the weight of hidden knowledge. I found myself pulled further into the heart of the arcane repository.

Among the dusty volumes, my eyes fell upon texts obscured by the passage of centuries. Grimoires, bound in leather weathered by time, whispered promises of realms beyond mortal comprehension. The shelves, though static, resonated with the echoes of forgotten incantations, and as I uncovered each obscure text, the boundaries between reality and the arcane blurred.

In the waking world, I reveled in the tactile exploration of these arcane treasures, but little did I know that my discoveries reverberated through Fantasia, where Aria perceived the subtle vibrations of each unveiled secret.

In Fantasia, where reality bent to the whims of the cosmic tapestry, Aria Evernight perceived the unfolding narrative with spectral clarity. The dimly lit aisles, existing as both a tangible and ethereal space, echoed with Daniel's discoveries.

The hidden tomes, discovered by Daniel in the waking world, manifested in Fantasia as radiant volumes adorned with eldritch symbols. Each revelation, each page turned, sent ripples through the Dreamlands. Aria, existing beyond the confines of physicality, marveled at the interplay between Daniel's mortal journey and the ethereal echoes in Fantasia.

As Daniel uncovered obscure texts, the boundaries between realms blurred. Fantasia responded to the vibrational dance initiated by his exploration. Eldritch entities, drawn to the resonance of ancient wisdom, stirred within the Dreamlands. Aria perceived the whispers of forgotten realms, each revealing a secret, a harmonic note in the cosmic symphony that unfolded between the waking world and Fantasia.

In the waking world, my hands traced the contours of hidden grimoires, blissfully unaware of the symbiotic dance echoing in Fantasia. As I unraveled the mysteries within the occult bookstore, Aria, in her spectral form, bore witness to the ethereal manifestations of arcane knowledge.

The very act of unveiling hidden knowledge became a bridge between realms. In the waking world, I immersed myself in the tangible exploration of arcane secrets. At the same time, Aria perceived the metaphysical resonance in Fantasia, her essence intertwining with the echoes of forgotten realms.

Aria, attuned to the cosmic forces, felt the stirrings of eldritch entities in Fantasia. Each revealed secret, each grimoire unearthed, beckoned forth ancient beings from the Dreamlands. The symbiosis deepened as the arcane knowledge unveiled in the occult bookstore became a beacon that guided eldritch forces through the metaphysical corridors of Fantasia.

In the dimly lit aisles, as I reveled in the tactile exploration of hidden knowledge, the symbiotic dance between realms intensified. Unseen forces orchestrated the unfolding narrative, where the tangible and the intangible danced harmoniously. The occult bookstore, existing both in the waking world and Fantasia, became a nexus of cosmic convergence, where the revelations of forgotten wisdom bound Aria's spectral essence with my mortal journey in a cosmic waltz.

—

In the dimly lit aisles of the occult bookstore, where ancient tomes beckoned with promises of forgotten knowledge, Daniel Eldrith's curiosity ignited like a flame in the dark. Among the shelves lined with cryptic symbols and the musty scent of untold tales, his eyes fell upon a book that seemed to pulse with otherworldly energy— "The Everlasting Nightmare."

The cover, a weathered tapestry of enigmatic symbols, seemed to writhe with a life of its own. Fingers tracing the edges, Daniel felt an unspoken connection, a call from realms beyond mortal understanding. The arcane symbols danced beneath his touch, revealing glimpses of eldritch secrets within its pages.

An almost imperceptible hum filled the air as Daniel delved into the tome's pages. The flickering candles cast shadows that seemed to whisper ancient secrets, echoing the cosmic vibrations hidden within the book's binding. Each word read tightened the bond between Daniel and the eldritch narrative, drawing him into a cosmic dance that transcended the boundaries of the waking world.

In Fantasia, the reflection of the occult bookstore mirrored its waking counterpart. Ethereal shelves held spectral tomes; among them, "The Everlasting Nightmare" radiated with an otherworldly luminescence. Aria, the Dreamweaver attuned to the echoes of the waking world, perceived Daniel's discoveries as ripples in the fabric of Fantasia.

In the Dreamlands, the book's cover transformed into a shifting tapestry of eldritch symbols, radiating an ethereal glow. With her spectral gaze, Aria beheld the book as a conduit between realms, its pulsating essence whispering the tale of cosmic disturbances. The Dreamweaver sensed the connection between mortal and narrative, a dance of destiny in which she played an unforeseen role.

As Daniel turned the pages, the ethereal echoes of the narrative reverberated through Fantasia. Aria perceived the cosmic vibrations, each word resonating with an ancient truth that transcended the Dreamlands. The connection deepened, an intangible thread binding Aria's spectral essence to the mortal who, unknowingly, had become a harbinger of cosmic disturbances.

In the waking world, Daniel's gaze remained fixed on the pages of "The Everlasting Nightmare." Unbeknownst to him, the symbiotic connection formed between the book and his mortal essence was echoed in Fantasia. Aria, the Dreamweaver, perceived the unraveling narrative with a spectral awareness that surpassed the limitations of the physical realm.

With every word read, the dance between realms intensified. The occult bookstore, a nexus of metaphysical convergence, became a stage for a cosmic waltz where mortal and spectral essences entwined. "The Everlasting Nightmare" was not merely a book; it was a key to a cosmic symphony, and as Daniel continued reading, the echoes of its revelations rippled through Fantasia, where Aria awaited the cosmic crescendo that would bind their fates inextricably.

Unbeknownst to both Daniel and Aria, the cosmic disturbance woven within the pages of "The Everlasting Nightmare" began to thread unseen strands through the fabric of their destinies. The eldritch symphony played on, and the dance of mortal and Dreamweaver became an intricate tapestry of intertwining fates, with each turn of the page drawing them closer to a cosmic revelation.

As I immersed myself in the eldritch tapestry of "The Everlasting Nightmare," a shadow loomed over the shelves, its presence undeniable. The Necronomicon, a tome infamous for its malevolent aura, stood as a sentinel of forbidden knowledge. Its leather-bound cover, adorned with cryptic symbols, seemed to writhe with an unspoken malevolence.

When my eyes met the Necronomicon, a shiver coursed through my spine. Its presence eclipsed the surrounding volumes, casting an oppressive atmosphere that echoed with whispers from distant cosmic realms. The air seemed to thicken as if acknowledging the ancient power contained within those pages.

"The Everlasting Nightmare" and the Necronomicon shared an eerie resonance, their mystical energies intertwining in an esoteric dance. Each word read in the former echoed through the latter, as if the eldritch narratives within both books were intertwined, dancing in tandem to a cosmic rhythm. It was as if the air around them pulsed with a malevolent heartbeat, revealing a hidden connection transcending the boundaries of mortal understanding.

In Fantasia, the reflection of the occult bookstore stretched into the Dreamlands. The spectral shelves held mirrored tomes; among them, the Necronomicon emanated a palpable malevolence. Aria, attuned to the echoes of eldritch knowledge, sensed the Necronomicon's ominous presence, a dark echo mirroring its counterpart in the waking world.

In the Dreamlands, the Necronomicon's cover seemed to pulsate with an otherworldly malevolence. Aria's spectral form regarded it with a mixture of caution and intrigue. The eldritch energies emanating from the tome cast an ethereal shadow, distorting the dreamlike landscapes around it. Fantasia, too, acknowledged the ominous significance of this ancient grimoire.

As Daniel continued his exploration of "The Everlasting Nightmare," the Necronomicon in Fantasia echoed with eldritch vibrations. The malevolent dance between the two tomes reverberated through the Dreamlands, creating a symphony of dark resonance in eerie harmony. Aria perceived the unholy synchronicity, sensing that the destinies of mortal and Dreamweaver were now entwined with the cosmic narrative and the malevolent echoes of forbidden knowledge.

In the waking world, the shadows cast by the Necronomicon seemed to dance with a newfound intensity. Unbeknownst to me, the malevolent energies within the forbidden grimoire responded to the cosmic disturbances woven within "The Everlasting Nightmare." The dance of dark resonance intensified, and the unseen threads that bound mortal and Dreamweaver began to weave a tapestry of eldritch destiny that transcended the boundaries of both realms. The air within the occult bookstore crackled with an unspoken anticipation, echoing the dark secrets hidden within the ancient tomes.

The flickering candles in the occult bookstore cast dancing shadows across the pages of "The Everlasting Nightmare" as I stood at the precipice of a decision that would alter the course of my reality. The eldritch whispers within the ancient grimoire beckoned me, each word pulling me deeper into the cosmic abyss. The weight of the tome in my hands felt like a bridge between the mundane and the unknown.

As I traced my fingers over the embossed cover of "The Everlasting Nightmare," a surge of conflicting emotions washed over me. The curiosity that fueled my academic pursuits collided with a subtle undercurrent of trepidation. Yet, the call of the unknown resonated with a magnetic pull, urging me to unravel the secrets concealed within its pages.

I opened the book with a determined breath, and the air seemed to ripple with anticipation. The first words leaped off the pages, weaving a tapestry of eldritch revelations that ensnared my consciousness. The allure of forbidden knowledge mingled with the ever-present sense of trepidation, creating a potent cocktail of emotions that fueled my journey into the heart of the cosmic nightmare.

—

In Fantasia, the resonance of Daniel's decision echoed through the Dreamlands. The pages of "The Everlasting Nightmare" contrasted with their waking-world counterpart, creating a harmonious dance between realms. Aria, existing on the ethereal plane, sensed the ripples of Daniel's choice as they reverberated through the fabric of Fantasia.

As the mortal Daniel delved into the cosmic narrative, the very essence of Fantasia quivered in response. The choices made by those bound to the waking world cast echoes into the Dreamlands, intertwining the destinies of Dreamweaver and mortal in a delicate dance of cosmic consequence.

The ink on the pages of "The Everlasting Nightmare" seemed to bleed into the very fabric of Fantasia. Aria observed the unfolding narrative, the choices made by the mortal resonating as ethereal threads woven into the tapestry of the Dreamlands. The unseen connections tightened, binding the fate of realms beyond mortal comprehension.

As I delved deeper into the eldritch revelations, the boundaries between the waking world and Fantasia blurred. The words on the pages seemed to transcend mere ink and parchment, reaching into the very essence of Fantasia. With each turned page, the convergence of realities became more palpable, and the cosmic dance between mortal and Dreamweaver unfolded in harmonious synchronicity.

Chapter 3
Unearthly Beginnings

I turned the pages of "The Everlasting Nightmare," expecting the mundane revelations of spells and incantations. My fingers traced over ancient symbols, and my eyes scanned the intricate diagrams, searching for the familiar rhythms of conventional magic.

In the dimly lit room, surrounded by the occult ambiance, I held on to the belief that "The Everlasting Nightmare" was nothing more than a conduit for traditional arcane knowledge. The weight of expectation mingled with the scent of old parchment as I anticipated the unveiling of age-old spells.

The text revealed itself in cryptic patterns as I scanned the pages. I muttered incantations under my breath, attempting to decipher the eldritch language woven into the very fabric of the narrative. Yet, with each passing moment, the realization dawned that this tome transcended the boundaries of conventional magic.

In Fantasia, the echoes of Daniel's anticipation resonated through the Dreamlands. The expectations he carried rippled through the tapestry of ethereal reality, creating subtle disturbances in the cosmic currents that shaped Fantasia's landscapes.

As the mortal Daniel grappled with his assumptions, the essence of Fantasia responded to the echoes of his expectations. Aria, attuned to the subtle shifts in the Dreamlands, sensed the ripples of anticipation. The ethereal plane vibrated with the echoes of his quest for knowledge, intertwining the threads of their destinies even further.

The ink on the pages of "The Everlasting Nightmare" seemed to react to Daniel's shifting perception. What he sought in conventional magic became a veil, slowly lifting to reveal the eldritch revelations that awaited him. Aria observed, her ethereal form resonating with the unfolding cosmic narrative as Daniel delved into the unknown depths of Fantasia's secrets.

The pages beneath my fingertips transformed, and the ink danced with ethereal luminescence. The symbols, once cryptic, now seemed to whisper ancient secrets directly into my mind. The air in the occult bookstore thickened with otherworldly energy as I immersed myself further into the cosmic narrative.

As if guided by an unseen force, my perception shifted. What I initially thought was a mere spell book was unfurled into a cosmic tapestry of Eldritch revelations. The boundaries of my understanding expanded, and I felt the subtle tendrils of the Dreamlands weaving into the fabric of my reality.

With each turned page, a cosmic invitation unfolded. It was as if the narrative itself reached out, drawing me into a realm beyond the confines of mortal expectations. The once-diminished expectations gave way to a hunger for the unknown. I willingly followed the beckoning call of the cosmic forces hidden within "The Everlasting Nightmare."

In Fantasia, Daniel's shifting perception echoes resonated with a melody that only ethereal beings could perceive. The Dreamlands responded to the cosmic invitation, harmonizing its landscapes with Daniel's newfound understanding.

The echoes of Daniel's acceptance echoed through Fantasia like an ethereal symphony. The Dreamlands, entwined with the cosmic forces, sensed his willingness to transcend the mundane. Whispers of his journey spread through the fantastical realm, drawing the attention of Eldritch entities and shaping the contours of landscapes untouched by mortal hands.

Aria, existing at the intersection of mortal perception and ethereal reality, felt their destinies intertwine. The cosmic forces that guided Daniel's immersion into the narrative reached across the veil, leaving ripples in Fantasia's dreamscape. The cosmic invitation became a shared experience, binding Aria and Daniel in a dance between mortal curiosity and eldritch revelation.

As my perception delved deeper into the cosmic tapestry woven by "The Everlasting Nightmare," a new figure emerged from the shadows of the narrative. Aria Evernight, a name that resonated like an echo in the vast expanse of the Dreamlands, became the focal point of the unfolding tale.

With each revelation, Aria materialized before the canvas of my imagination. She stood as a lone figure against the cosmic backdrop, her silhouette painted with mystery and enigma. Aria, a beacon in the ethereal darkness, beckoned me to witness her journey through the realms of Fantasia.

Her enigmatic qualities stirred my curiosity. Aria Evernight, a mortal in the waking world, held a presence that transcended the ordinary. In Fantasia, where dreams took tangible form, Aria navigated the shifting landscapes with an otherworldly grace. Like the pages of the cosmic narrative, her existence bore the weight of eldritch revelations yet to be unveiled.

In Fantasia, where dreams intertwined with the fabric of reality, Aria sensed Daniel's gaze piercing through the veil that separated their worlds. The Dreamlands responded to his curiosity. Aria became aware of the mortal who dared to peer into the cosmic tapestry she called home.

The Dreamlands whispered of a mortal, Daniel Eldritch, whose perception transcended the ordinary. Aria, a Dreamweaver in the cosmic tale, felt the threads of mortal curiosity weaving into the very essence of Fantasia. His gaze, though distant, became a subtle undercurrent in the symphony of dreams that painted the landscapes around Aria.

Aria, in her enigmatic existence, acknowledged the connection. Mortal and ethereal, Daniel and Aria danced on the delicate boundary between waking reality and fantastical dreams. Though unknown to her, his presence added a layer of complexity to the cosmic narrative that unfolded with every turn of the page.

As I delved further into "The Everlasting Nightmare," the ethereal landscapes of Fantasia unfolded before my mind's eye. It was a realm of fractured dreams and shattered realities, where the rules of existence danced on the precipice of chaos. Fantasia, a tapestry woven from the dreams of a slumbering god, held both the allure of enchantment and the terror of cosmic unraveling.

Surreal dimensions stretched endlessly, disorienting the senses as the fabric of Fantasia trembled under the disturbance. Mountains twisted into grotesque shapes, and rivers flowed in defiance of gravity. Each step through Fantasia was a journey into the unknown, where the ground beneath my feet whispered of Eldritch's secrets yet unveiled.

In the heart of Fantasia, where dreams materialized, and fragmented realities merged, Aria sensed the subtle intrusion of an outsider's perception. The Dreamlands, woven from the slumbering god's dreams, responded to the echoes of Daniel's curiosity, casting ripples through the very essence of Fantasia.

Fantasia, in all its bewitching allure, bore the scars of a cosmic disturbance. Shattered landscapes unfolded like a tapestry unraveling at the seams. Mountains contorted into nightmarish shapes, and rivers flowed in defiance of the conventional laws that bound the waking world. As a Dreamweaver, Aria traversed these surreal dimensions, navigating the fractured realities that mirrored the disturbance within the Dreamlands.

As the disturbance in the cosmic narrative echoed through Fantasia, Aria felt the disorienting currents of the slumbering god's dreams. The very fabric of Fantasia trembled, and the once-stable landscapes crumbled into kaleidoscopic disarray. Each step carried the weight of cosmic uncertainty. Aria danced on the fringes of reality, teetering on the edge of madness.

As I delved deeper into the eldritch narrative within "The Everlasting Nightmare," a peculiar awareness dawned upon me. The words I consumed on each page resonated beyond the confines of paper and ink. I began to comprehend that my reading wasn't a passive act but a communion with the cosmic forces dictating Fantasia's destiny. Each interpretation, each nuance in my perception, wove into the fabric of Aria's journey.

With every turned page, I sensed an ethereal thread connecting my thoughts to Aria's footsteps in Fantasia. The symbiotic nature of our connection became undeniable. The landscapes she traversed responded to the cadence of my understanding, and the cosmic disturbance echoed with the harmonies of our intertwined fates. Fantasia reflected my comprehension, an intricate dance between reader and narrative.

In Fantasia's surreal expanse, Aria perceived the subtle currents of an unseen force. Whispers of Daniel's realizations echoed through the Dreamlands like notes of an eldritch melody. As a Dreamweaver, she felt the ebb and flow of the symbiotic connection, realizing that the intruder in her dreams held the key to the unraveling cosmic tapestry.

As Daniel's understanding expanded, Aria felt the resonance within Fantasia's essence. The landscapes shifted, responding to the nuances of his comprehension. She became attuned to the pulse of his thoughts, a dance of consciousness that echoed in the dreamscape. It was a delicate balance, and Aria, ever the weaver of realities, understood that their connection held the power to shape the destiny of both realms.

Chapter 4
Eldritch Entities Awaken

Once a realm of harmonious dreams, Fantasia now resonated with discordant echoes. As I traversed its shattered landscapes, the very fabric of the Dreamlands quivered with unease. The once serene Dreamweaver's Haven now echoed with the dissonant strains of eldritch disturbance, weaving nightmares into the tapestry of Fantasia's reality.

The awakening echoed through the surreal corridors, calling forth entities that slumbered in the shadowy corners of Fantasia. Eldritch beings, with forms transcending mortal comprehension, stirred from their dormant states. As I faced these entities, their alien presence seeped into my consciousness, revealing the depths of their disturbance. They were manifestations of the Dreamlands' turmoil, unsettling yet integral to understanding the cosmic unraveling.

With each turned page, I observed the metamorphosis of Fantasia through Aria's eyes. The once serene landscapes twisted into surreal nightmares, mirroring the awakening of eldritch entities within the Dreamlands. As an inadvertent architect of this transformation, I grappled with the consequences of my symbiotic connection with Aria and the cosmic narrative.

The eldritch entities, born of Fantasia's disruption, manifested as grotesque amalgamations of nightmare and reality. Through Aria's encounters, I witnessed the dance between Dreamweaver and entity, a delicate balance disrupted by the cosmic disturbance. Fantasia, a canvas painted with eldritch hues, bore the scars of awakening entities, their presence echoing through the symbiotic connection that bound Aria and me.

The eldritch entities, once mere whispers in the cosmic winds, had now materialized into grotesque forms defying mortal comprehension. Each entity seemed to embody the essence of cosmic horror, their twisted limbs and shifting forms reflecting the profound disturbance in Fantasia. As I faced these eldritch beings, their presence painted a nightmarish canvas within the Dreamlands, echoing the disharmony that permeated the once-serene realm.

The first entity, Nyctalus, manifested as a shadowy amalgamation of ethereal tendrils. Its form undulated with an otherworldly grace, resonating with the eerie echoes of the cosmic disturbance. The second, Azathoth's Whisperer, resembled a distorted symphony of maddening whispers, each utterance carrying the weight of forgotten nightmares. These beings, now awakened, personified the chaos that threatened to consume Fantasia.

Amid this eldritch awakening, I was entangled in a dance with nightmares given life. Their malevolence tested my resolve as a Dreamweaver, pushing the limits of my ability to shape the dreams that fueled Fantasia. The symbiotic connection, once a conduit of understanding, now resonated with the discord of the entities' emergence.

Nyctalus's tendrils wove through the fabric of my carefully crafted dreams, leaving behind threads of corruption. Azathoth's Whisperer echoed haunting melodies that threatened to unravel the very essence of Fantasia. The once harmonious dance of dreams had devolved into a cacophony of cosmic disharmony.

Through the pages of "The Everlasting Nightmare," I delved into Aria's struggles against these eldritch entities. Each entity, a brushstroke of cosmic horror, painted a surreal tapestry within Fantasia. Aria's reactions mirrored my internal turmoil, the consequences of my unwitting influence on the Dreamlands unfolding vividly.

The descriptions within the narrative were vivid, each a testament to the indescribable horror lurking in the corners of Fantasia. Nyctalus's presence oozed from the pages, its tendrils reaching out to intertwine with my growing awareness. Azathoth's Whisperer, its haunting melodies, echoed through the written words, transcending the boundaries between fiction and reality.

Aria's struggle against the eldritch beings resonated with my own awakening awareness. The once-static words on the pages now pulsed with the living essence of cosmic disturbance. The symbiotic connection intensified, blurring the lines between narrator and character, reader and protagonist. Fantasia's fate and ours are inexplicably intertwined in the cosmic struggle against awakened nightmares.

The realization dawned that the eldritch entities, unleashed by the disturbance in the Dreamlands, were not mere products of fiction but living embodiments of the cosmic disharmony Daniel had unwittingly unleashed upon Fantasia. Once a whimsical exploration, the struggle for control over the narrative now became a desperate battle against the nightmares that threatened to spill into reality.

The dim glow of the reading lamp cast a spectral hue on "The Everlasting Nightmare" pages as I continued my journey through Aria's cosmic struggles. The once-familiar act of reading became a portal, a bridge between the waking world and Fantasia, each word a ripple in the fabric of reality.

The realization gripped me, a cold hand squeezing my heart. Every nuance of emotion within Aria's encounters mirrored the subtle shifts in my consciousness. The symbiotic link, at first a curious connection, now revealed its true nature—a conduit between realms woven by the threads of narrative influence.

As Nyctalus extended its tendrils in Fantasia, I felt the ethereal touch brushing against my thoughts. The eldritch resonance reverberated within, acknowledging my inadvertent role in shaping the cosmic disharmony. The narrative had become a living entity, responding to my interpretations with eldritch entities that mirrored the turmoil of Fantasia.

I witnessed the consequences unfold like a cosmic tapestry with each page-turn. Azathoth's Whisperer, the embodiment of forgotten nightmares, echoed its malevolent melodies within the confines of "The Everlasting Nightmare." The words seemed to pulse with eldritch energy, their influence extending beyond the pages and into the fabric of Fantasia.

In my quiet study, I felt the echoes of Aria's struggles reverberating. Fantasia and the waking world were no longer separate entities. The ripple effect of my reading extended far beyond the confines of the dimly lit room. Eldritch entities danced on the precipice of reality, their manifestations driven by the symbiotic link between the narrative and my unwitting influence.

Reading had transformed into an act of creation, and I, the unwitting architect of cosmic disturbance. The boundary between fiction and reality blurred, and the consequences of my literary exploration unfolded in ways I could scarcely comprehend.

In the shifting planes of Fantasia, where reality and dreams intertwined, Aria Evernight navigated the fractured landscapes, unaware of the unseen hand guiding her fate.

As I treaded through the shattered realms of Fantasia, echoes of forgotten dreams whispered through the air. Unbeknownst to me, Daniel's readings resonated in the unseen currents, shaping the very fabric of this eldritch tapestry. The Dreamlands, once stable, now quivered with unsettling energy, responding to the unintentional disturbances wrought by Daniel's exploration of "The Everlasting Nightmare."

Eldritch entities, drawn forth by the influence of Daniel's interpretations, emerged as malevolent specters in my path. Azathoth's Whisperer, a creature born of Daniel's subconscious musings, haunted the edges of my perception. Each note of its cosmic symphony echoed with the unintended consequences of Daniel's readings, distorting the very essence of Fantasia.

Every turn of the page in the waking world translated to a seismic shift within Fantasia. The entities, once dormant, stirred with a newfound malevolence, their existence now intertwined with the inked words of "The Everlasting Nightmare." Daniel's influence, a silent force shaping the narrative, reached beyond the confines of his study, bleeding into the very foundations of this surreal realm.

The cosmic balance, delicate and precarious, tipped under the weight of Daniel's unintended manipulations. Aria Evernight, unaware of the invisible threads weaving her destiny, faced challenges that mirrored the turmoil of the waking world. Eldritch adversaries, born of Daniel's unwitting conjurations, manifested with an insidious purpose, their actions guided by the silent whispers of a reader lost in the cosmic dance.

In the interplay of fiction and reality, Aria and Daniel found themselves bound by an intricate dance—a dance where each step in the waking world resonated in the ethereal landscapes of Fantasia, and every movement within Fantasia reverberated through the quiet study where Daniel delved deeper into the pages of "The Everlasting Nightmare."

As the weight of every turned page bore down on my conscience, I couldn't escape the disquieting realization that my journey into "The Everlasting Nightmare" wasn't a solitary endeavor. Aria Evernight, the central character within these inked realms, faced challenges not of her own making. Fantasia responded to my very presence in ways I never anticipated.

In the muted glow of my study, I read on, oblivious to the unfolding drama in the realms beyond the text. In her ceaseless exploration of Fantasia, Aria encountered echoes of my musings. The eldritch entities, drawn forth by my interpretations, mirrored my emotional landscape, their actions weaving a tapestry that connected reader and protagonist inextricably.

Aria felt the echoes of my thoughts as I deciphered the arcane words within the pages. Each line etched in ink shaped her destiny, and every inflection of my imagination resonated within the shifting landscapes of Fantasia. The symbiotic connection formed an unbroken thread, blurring the lines between author and character as the cosmic dance continued.

—

In the kaleidoscopic expanse of Fantasia, the lines between reality and fiction blurred, and I found myself ensnared in the unseen web woven by Daniel's interpretations. The eldritch entities, now driven by the rhythm of his thoughts, responded to the silent dance between us.

Once a realm governed by its enigmatic laws, Fantasia now bore the fingerprints of a distant reader.

The boundaries between Daniel's world and mine disintegrated, and the narrative became a living, breathing entity influenced by the musings of an unwitting conductor.

In this convergence, I felt the ebb and flow of Daniel's emotions, the resonance of his fears and hopes reverberating through the very essence of Fantasia. The cosmic narrative, a dance of interwoven destinies, threw us into a maelstrom where roles blurred, and the distinction between observer and participant became increasingly elusive.

As I faced the eldritch entities, their malevolence amplified by the unintended consequences of a reader's journey, I couldn't shake the feeling that Daniel and I were on a collision course with a reality where the boundaries of fiction and existence merged into a singular, cosmic tapestry.

Part II
Threads of Fate

Chapter 5
Whispers of Entanglement

The nights blurred into one another as I delved ever deeper into the eldritch tapestry that "The Everlasting Nightmare" unfurled before me. The lines between the waking world and the cosmic realms within the book began to blur. I found myself entangled in a narrative transcending mere storytelling's boundaries.

The flickering candlelight cast dancing shadows across the pages, each word resonating with an eldritch energy that both fascinated and unnerved me. My curiosity morphed into a relentless pursuit, each paragraph a breadcrumb leading me further into the labyrinth of cosmic horrors and tangled destinies.

With every passing chapter, the threads of fate binding me to Fantasia tightened. The symbiotic connection grew more profound, and the eldritch entities within the pages mirrored my journey. It was as if the book itself had become a sentient being, responding to my emotions, fears, and desires with a cosmic dance transcending mere fiction's boundaries.

As I navigated the labyrinthine corridors of the eldritch tale, I couldn't escape the feeling that the beings within were aware of my presence, as if they, too, were reading the words etched on the parchment of their existence. Fantasia, once a distant and fantastical realm, now felt like a reflection of my psyche, each turn of the page shaping not only their destinies but mine.

—

In the ever-shifting landscapes of Fantasia, the echoes of Daniel's explorations manifested as spectral whispers, guiding my steps. The eldritch entities, once mere manifestations of ink and imagination, now pulsed with a vitality influenced by Daniel's insatiable curiosity.

As I traversed the surreal landscapes, a shadowy figure emerged—a winged silhouette named Nyctalus. This enigmatic ally, a product of Daniel's exploration, guided me through the cosmic narrative. The unseen threads of fate wove a tapestry that connected us, transcending the boundaries of reader and protagonist.

Nyctalus, a herald of the eldritch symphony, whispered secrets of the unfolding cosmic drama. The symbiotic connection between Daniel and me became more palpable, and the threads that bound our destinies intertwined, creating a dance of cosmic significance.

Temporal anomalies manifested, distorting the fabric of Fantasia. Daniel's persistent exploration echoed through the fragmented realities, and I found myself caught in a kaleidoscope of timelines that mirrored his journey. The threads of fate pulled tighter, and the cosmic narrative reached a crescendo where the distinction between us became increasingly elusive.

As Daniel continued his relentless exploration, the whispers of entanglement grew louder, and the cosmic symphony echoed with the shared melodies of our destinies. The eldritch tale, now a living entity shaped by the interplay of reader and protagonist, beckoned us further into its cosmic embrace.

The resonance of the eldritch symphony echoed through the pages of "The Everlasting Nightmare." With each word, Daniel felt the pulse of Fantasia quicken. The symbiotic connection between his reading and the unfolding events within the cosmic tale intensified. Every nuance, every emotion etched in the narrative, seemed to ripple through the fabric of Fantasia.

As I wandered through the ever-shifting landscapes, the echoes of Daniel's exploration manifested in ethereal whispers. The eldritch entities, now attuned to Daniel's presence, responded to the cadence of his reading, their forms undulating in response to the cosmic vibrations.

The threads of fate binding us together tightened, and Daniel's growing awareness became a beacon within the fragmented realities of Fantasia. His curiosity, fears, and hopes materialized as spectral threads that wove through the very fabric of this surreal realm.

As Daniel's understanding of the cosmic narrative deepened, so did the challenges within Fantasia. Eldritch adversaries, drawn by the symbiotic connection, materialized as manifestations of his thoughts and fears. They roamed the shattered landscapes, embodying the darker echoes of his exploration.

These symbiotic nightmares, fueled by the resonance of the eldritch symphony, cast shadows over Fantasia. Their malevolent presence mirrored the complexities of Daniel's psyche, and the boundary between reader and protagonist blurred further.

The nightmares began to roam freely, born from the synergy between Daniel's reading and the eldritch entities. Their movements synchronized with the cadence of the cosmic disturbance, creating a nightmarish symphony that echoed through Fantasia. Each step and encounter bore the indelible mark of Daniel's influence.

As Daniel grappled with the consequences of his reading, I, too, faced the repercussions in Fantasia. Once a subtle dance, the symbiotic connection has now evolved into a frenetic ballet of intertwined destinies. The boundary between reader and protagonist blurred further, and the cosmic forces at play intensified as the threads of fate tightened, pulling us deeper into the tapestry of the Everlasting Nightmare.

The eldritch symphony echoed through the realms, its resonance weaving the destinies of Aria and Daniel ever closer. As Daniel's influence in Fantasia grew, so did the unpredictable dance between our worlds.

Aria wandered through the surreal landscapes of Fantasia, where the echoes of Daniel's exploration manifested in surreal distortions. Shadows shifted, and the air seemed charged with the energy of his thoughts. The symbiotic connection, once a mere undercurrent, now manifested in unexpected crossroads where our paths intersected.

Within the tapestry of Fantasia, I conversed with eldritch entities drawn to the unfolding cosmic tale. Their voices, cryptic and laden with cosmic wisdom, spoke of threads that bound us together. These unseen strands wove through the fabric of realities, guiding Aria and Daniel along paths that resonated with the eldritch symphony.

The temporal anomalies within Fantasia became more pronounced. Moments unfolded out of sequence, and fragmented realities revealed glimpses of forgotten histories. The eldritch entities, emissaries of the cosmic disturbance, urged us to follow the echoes—the whispers of forgotten dreams that bridged the gap between our worlds.

Guided by the enigmatic entities, Aria and Daniel followed the echoes, unraveling the layers of their shared destiny. The boundaries between Fantasia and the waking world blurred as the connection threads tightened. Eldritch allies and adversaries became narrators in this cosmic tale, their voices resonating harmoniously with the eldritch symphony.

The dance of threads and echoes led us toward a convergence, where the cosmic forces at play became palpable. The intricate tapestry of the Everlasting Nightmare unfurled, revealing the interconnectedness of our fates amidst the chaos and beauty of the eldritch saga.

Aria's journey through Fantasia took an ominous turn as a particularly formidable symbiotic nightmare emerged from the cosmic tapestry. Its form echoed the distortions in Daniel's waking world, a nightmarish reflection of challenges yet to come.

Aria faced this eldritch behemoth, its existence entwined with the echoes of Daniel's struggles. The battleground mirrored Daniel's waking world challenges, and Aria confronted not just a creature born of cosmic disturbance but the essence of Daniel's fears and trials.

Meanwhile, in the waking world, Daniel encountered challenges that mirrored Aria's nightmarish confrontation. The dance between realms intensified as the connection between Fantasia and reality blurred further. Daniel's steps resonated within the eldritch symphony, amplifying Aria's struggles.

The symbiotic link reached a point where the boundaries between our experiences became indistinguishable. Aria's confrontation with the nightmare echoed in Daniel's waking world and vice versa. The cosmic forces orchestrating this dance reached a crescendo, weaving our fates more intricately than ever before.

As the symphony played, the dance of nightmares unfolded, pushing Aria and Daniel to the limits of their endurance. The eldritch presence deepened, and the cosmic tapestry unraveled, revealing the following movements in this cosmic saga.

—

In the wake of the dance of nightmares, a new chapter unfolded for Daniel Eldritch. The eldritch forces, recognizing his pivotal role in the cosmic narrative, introduced Nyctalus—an ethereal guide manifesting as shadows in the waking world. Nyctalus, a specter of ancient knowledge, guided Daniel through the labyrinthine passages of "The Everlasting Nightmare."

As Nyctalus weaved through the eldritch symphony, cryptic visions unraveled before Daniel's eyes. The narrative threads danced, revealing the interconnected fates of Aria, Daniel, and the eldritch entities. The symbiotic connection between the realms intensified. Daniel found himself not merely reading the cosmic tale but actively participating in its unfolding.

—

In Fantasia, Aria Evernight sensed the emergence of Nyctalus. The eldritch guide cast shadows across the surreal landscapes, leaving echoes of cryptic insights. Aria's path intertwined with Nyctalus's guidance, and she felt the resonance of Daniel's presence within the cosmic symphony.

As the eldritch allies and adversaries danced in tandem, the threads of fate tightened. Aria's journey became an intricate part of Daniel's exploration, and the eldritch symphony echoed their shared visions. Sensing the convergence of destinies, the eldritch forces whispered enigmatic truths that urged them to delve deeper into the cosmic unraveling.

Aria and Daniel, in separate realms yet bound by the eldritch symphony, experienced shared visions. The echoes of forgotten dreams whispered cryptic messages, bridging the gap between Fantasia and the waking world. Eldritch entities provided enigmatic guidance, their voices echoing through the cosmic tapestry, urging Aria and Daniel to follow the echoes toward an uncertain destiny.

The eldritch symphony played on, its haunting melody guiding the protagonists towards a convergence of realities that held the key to unraveling the cosmic mysteries.

—

Guided by Nyctalus through the cosmic threads, Daniel delved deeper into the eldritch symphony. The veil between Fantasia and the waking world trembled as the symbiotic connection reached a critical point. Nyctalus, the spectral guide, became a conduit for the intricate melodies of the cosmic narrative, unveiling cryptic insights into the unraveling destinies.

Daniel felt the weight of his role in the cosmic design as the eldritch allies whispered enigmatic truths. The symbiotic connection intensified, pushing him to the limits of his understanding. Eldritch forces offered cryptic insights into the impending chaos, and Daniel sensed that the unraveling of realities was inevitable.

—

In Fantasia, Aria Evernight felt the echoes of Nyctalus's guidance. Eldritch adversaries, drawn to the symbiotic connection, manifested as nightmarish symphonies roaming the shattered landscapes. The veil of madness thickened, blurring the boundaries between dreams and nightmares.

Aria confronted formidable symbiotic nightmares, each reflecting the eldritch disturbance echoing from Daniel's exploration. The cosmic forces entwined them further. Aria navigated through the increasingly distorted realities, her every step echoing in Daniel's waking world.

Aria and Daniel, facing challenges in their respective realms, felt the growing resonance of the eldritch symphony. The veil between their experiences wavered, and the cosmic forces manipulated the threads of fate, creating a nightmarish dance that echoed through Fantasia and the waking world.

As the protagonists approached the brink of the cosmic disturbance, the eldritch symphony played on, resonating through the realms, pushing Aria and Daniel to confront the madness that lurked beyond the veil.

Chapter 6
Echoes in Fantasia

As Aria traversed the shattered landscapes of Fantasia, an unsettling awareness crept into her senses. Whispers of external influence danced on the edges of her consciousness, elusive yet undeniable. The echoes of Daniel's exploration reverberated through the surreal dimensions, leaving traces of his presence in the cosmic tapestry.

The once-familiar nightmares took on a new resonance as if Daniel's interpretations bled into the very fabric of Fantasia. Aria found herself entangled in the threads of his exploration, each step she took influenced by the disturbances echoing from the waking world.

The air in Fantasia crackled with an ethereal tension as Aria delved deeper into the enigmatic echoes. Shadows stirred in response to Daniel's journey through "The Everlasting Nightmare," their spectral forms merging with the surreal landscape. Aria, usually the solitary traveler in her dreamlike realm, now felt the presence of unseen forces tugging at the strands of her existence.

Eldritch adversaries, drawn to the symbiotic connection between Aria and Daniel, manifested with heightened malevolence. The whispers of Daniel's influence attracted otherworldly entities, and Aria confronted the first signs of their emergence. These eldritch foes, born from the cosmic disturbance, sought to challenge Aria's resilience and disrupt the delicate balance within Fantasia.

From the shadows, grotesque shapes materialized, their forms a grotesque reflection of the nightmares Aria once navigated alone. The cosmic disturbance, fueled by Daniel's exploration, transformed these nightmares into formidable adversaries, each embodying a facet of the eldritch forces at play. Aria faced challenges not only from within but also from the external forces woven into the cosmic narrative.

As Aria ventured further, symbiotic nightmares materialized, mirroring the intricate dance of cosmic forces. These nightmares, a manifestation of the connection between Aria and Daniel, roamed the fragmented realities of Fantasia. Aria's perception of the world shifted, and the echoes of Daniel's exploration became more pronounced, leading her toward unforeseen challenges.

The symbiotic nightmares, now sentient and responsive to Daniel's journey, added a layer of complexity to Aria's odyssey. Each encounter with these manifestations brought her closer to understanding the interwoven destinies. Still, it also pushed her further into the surreal depths of the cosmic disturbance.

The boundaries between dream and reality blurred as Aria grappled with the escalating external influence. The eldritch adversaries sensed the symbiotic connection, drawing them closer to the unfolding cosmic tale that intertwined the destinies of Aria and Daniel. Once a realm shaped solely by Aria's dreams, Fantasia now resonated with the echoes of a narrative written by the waking world, creating a complex and enthralling web of eldritch intrigue.

—

As I immersed myself deeper into "The Everlasting Nightmare," the line between reader and protagonist blurred, and I sensed a profound connection forming between my exploration and Aria's journey through Fantasia. Every word I read seemed to reverberate through the cosmic threads, leaving an indelible mark on the surreal landscapes Aria navigated.

The eldritch guide, Nyctalus, whispered cryptic insights into the symbiotic nature of our odysseys. Through the ethereal entity's guidance, I began comprehending the intricate dance between reader and narrative, observer and participant. The echoes of my interpretation seeped into Fantasia, altering the essence of Aria's dreamscape.

—

In Fantasia, the once-stable dreamscapes twisted and contorted, responding to unseen forces at play. Shadows cast by Daniel's exploration manifested as living entities, their forms a reflection of the cosmic disturbances detailed in "The Everlasting Nightmare." As I walked through the fragmented realities, I encountered these manifestations, each step bringing me closer to the convergence of our destinies.

The eldritch adversaries, shaped by Daniel's interpretations, embodied the malevolence of the unseen forces at play. Their grotesque forms lurked in the shadows, challenging the harmony I once maintained within Fantasia. The nightmares, now infused with external influences, became a testament to the entanglement of our fates.

The symbiotic connection between the reader and the dreamer intensified. Fantasia, once Aria's sanctuary, transformed into a stage for the cosmic interplay between our journeys. Unseen forces, unleashed by my exploration, manifested as echoes that guided Aria through the shifting landscapes.

Aria grappled with the consequences of my reading, facing manifestations born from the eldritch tapestry woven into the waking world. The dreamscapes pulsed with energy, reacting to the twists and turns of "The Everlasting Nightmare," binding our narratives inextricably.

The very fabric of Fantasia underwent a metamorphosis, influenced by the external elements seeping into its essence. The once-pure dreamscape now bore the imprints of my interpretations, creating a surreal amalgamation of realities. Integrating these external elements added complexity to Aria's odyssey, challenging her understanding of the dreamlike realms she traversed.

As Fantasia evolved, shadows whispered secrets of the cosmic disturbance, revealing the intricate dance between the waking world and the dreamlands. The echoes of my reading became an integral part of Aria's journey, creating a tapestry where the boundaries between reader and protagonist dissolved, and the cosmic tale unfolded with each turn of the page.

—

In the shadowed realms of Fantasia, where echoes whispered and cosmic threads intertwined, I felt a disturbance drawing malevolence from the darkest corners of the eldritch tapestry. The once-harmonious dreamscape now resonated with a dissonant symphony, heralding the emergence of eldritch adversaries converging on my path.

As I wandered through surreal landscapes, the subtle ripples of Daniel's reading transformed into tangible manifestations. Eldritch adversaries, drawn by the cosmic rift he uncovered, slithered and materialized from the shadows. Their forms, a grotesque fusion of nightmare and eldritch malevolence, mirrored the chaos within the waking world.

—

The turning of the pages echoed through the eldritch realms, resonating with the stirrings of malevolence in Fantasia. The disturbance drew the attention of entities lurking on cosmic understanding fringes. As Aria traversed the dreamscapes, eldritch adversaries emerged to challenge her existence like shadows taking corporeal form.

Nyctalus, the ethereal guide, cryptically spoke of the convergence, where the eldritch disturbance and Aria's journey intersected. The malevolent entities, drawn to the cosmic rift forged by my reading, manifested with increasing intensity, casting long shadows over Aria's odyssey.

In Fantasia, the eldritch adversaries closed in, their nightmarish forms casting grotesque shadows upon the fragmented landscapes. The essence of the dreamlands twisted and contorted under the influence of these malevolent entities, each step I took further entwining my fate with their ominous presence.

As I read, an ominous realization dawned. Once a mere ripple in the cosmic fabric, the eldritch disturbance had become a beacon drawing forth ancient malevolence. The eldritch adversaries, born from the convergence of my exploration and Aria's journey, loomed more extensive, their purpose unfathomable, their gaze fixed on the dreamer in their midst.

The eldritch symphony played on, a dissonant melody weaving through the realms as shadows converged on Aria's path. The malevolent entities, drawn by the disturbance in the cosmic tapestry, became harbingers of a darker chapter in the unfolding cosmic tale.

—

The dreamlands quivered with malevolence as the eldritch adversaries, born from the convergence of cosmic disturbance and Daniel's reading, closed in. The once serene landscapes now echoed with dissonant whispers, and each step became a dance on the precipice of madness.

The eldritch adversaries, grotesque amalgamations of nightmare and otherworldly malevolence, confronted me at every turn. Each encounter tested my resolve, the shifting balance in Fantasia echoing the tumultuous symphony Daniel unknowingly composed. The veil between the realms trembled, and the eldritch adversaries became more than mere shadows—they embodied the nightmares lurking in the recesses of cosmic consciousness.

–

As I delved deeper into "The Everlasting Nightmare," the consequences of my actions unfolded. Eldritch adversaries, once ethereal whispers, manifested with a malevolent intent that reverberated through the dreamlands. Aria, my unwitting protagonist, faced a growing onslaught as the eldritch entities disrupted the delicate balance of Fantasia.

The fabric of reality in Fantasia shifted under the weight of these eldritch adversaries. Nightmares intertwined with Aria's journey, testing her resilience and sanity. Each struggle against these cosmic horrors became a crescendo in the eldritch symphony. This symphony unfolded in tandem with Daniel's reading.

The eldritch adversaries, their grotesque forms casting ominous shadows, intensified their assault. As I fought against the nightmares made flesh, the lines between sanity and madness blurred. The cosmic disturbance had reached a critical point, pushing both realms to chaos.

In the waking world, the flickering candles of the occult bookstore echo the wavering balance in Fantasia. The eldritch symphony, now a cacophony, resonated through every page turned. The consequences of my reading unfolded in Aria's descent into the nightmarish abyss.

The veil of madness draped over Fantasia, echoing my unwitting orchestration. The eldritch adversaries, once mere echoes, now manifested in grotesque detail. The shifting balance, disrupted by my exploration, bore witness to the unraveling cosmic tapestry. The dance between dream and reality reached a fevered pitch, and the symphony of madness crescendoed.

The echoes of Daniel's reading transformed into tangible nightmares, born from the symbiotic connection between his interpretations and the cosmic reality of Fantasia. Each nightmarish entity mirrored the twisted landscapes of Daniel's mind, and their emergence intensified the horror that enveloped me.

The once ethereal whispers now manifested as grotesque entities, stalking the surreal landscapes of Fantasia. As I traversed the otherworldly terrain, the symbiotic nightmares clawed at the very fabric of reality, their malevolence echoing the cosmic terrors unleashed by Daniel's unwitting influence.

My steps through Fantasia became a harrowing journey through a labyrinth of twisted nightmares. The symbiotic nightmares, now endowed with life through

Daniel's interpretation, manifested in forms beyond imagination. Eldritch tendrils coiled around phantasmal trees, and the sky seemed to bleed with otherworldly hues.

The eldritch symphony climaxed as the symbiotic nightmares prowled through the pages of "The Everlasting Nightmare." Every turn gave rise to new horrors, manifesting the symbiotic connection between my interpretations and the evolving cosmic narrative.

The once distinct realms of reader and protagonist blurred further. The nightmares, now living embodiments of my unwitting influence, roamed the dreamlands with a malevolent purpose. Each manifestation became a testament to the delicate dance between creator and creation, reader and protagonist.

As Daniel delved deeper into the eldritch tome, the symbiotic nightmares took on a palpable presence in the occult bookstore. Shadows morphed into eldritch entities, and whispers resonated with the eerie symphony. Daniel's surroundings mirrored the nightmarish landscapes in Fantasia, creating an unsettling parallel between the waking world and the dreamlands.

Fantasia became a nightmarish labyrinth twisted by symbiotic nightmares. As I navigated the surreal landscapes, the eldritch entities mirrored the horrors etched into the pages by Daniel's reading. The symbiotic nightmares whispered secrets of forgotten nightmares, their presence amplifying the cosmic disturbance.

The boundaries between dream and reality blurred, and I found myself ensnared in a symphony of madness. The symbiotic nightmares, influenced by

Daniel's exploration of the eldritch narrative, coalesced into an otherworldly force threatening to consume Fantasia and the waking world.

In the waking world, the occult bookstore echoed with the symphony of cosmic horrors. The symbiotic nightmares, now unleashed upon Fantasia, danced through each turned page. The delicate balance between the reader and the protagonist has unraveled completely. I realized that my interpretation was shaping Aria's descent into the abyss of madness.

The symbiotic nightmares, once confined to the pages of "The Everlasting Nightmare," now roamed freely through Fantasia. The eldritch symphony, now a cacophony of malevolence, intensified with every step Aria took, bringing the cosmic narrative to a precipice of chaos.

Daniel felt the weight of responsibility for the nightmares that spilled into Fantasia as he continued reading. The once passive act of interpreting the cosmic tale now felt like a dance on the edge of a reality-altering precipice. The eldritch entities in the occult bookstore seemed to respond to his every thought, blurring the line between creator and creation.

The symbiotic nightmares, once mere echoes of Daniel's interpretation, gained sentience. They whispered secrets of forgotten dreams, their forms evolving with each page turn. The eldritch symphony reverberating through the bookstore transcended the boundaries of imagination, entwining Daniel's waking world with Aria's nightmarish journey.

As the symbiotic nightmares manifested in Fantasia, Aria confronted the grotesque entities that mirrored Daniel's thoughts. The once beautiful landscapes of Fantasia now echoed with the wails of eldritch horrors. Aria's descent into madness mirrored Daniel's realization of the unintended consequences of his reading, creating a narrative dance between the two protagonists.

The eldritch symphony, a manifestation of Daniel's interpretation, resonated with the nightmares in both realms. Fantasia became a battleground where the consequences of reading unfolded in surreal proportions. Fueled by the cosmic disturbance, the symbiotic nightmares grew in strength, creating an intricate dance of malevolence that engulfed Aria and Daniel in a shared nightmare.

As Daniel grappled with the consequences of his reading, the occult bookstore transformed into a surreal reflection of Fantasia. Eldritch entities slithered between bookshelves, and the air vibrated with the echoes of the cosmic narrative. The symbiotic connection between the reader and the protagonist became an inescapable reality, blurring the boundaries between the waking world and the dreamlands.

Now aware of their connection to the reader's interpretation, the symbiotic nightmares took on a sentience that mirrored Daniel's growing understanding of their influence. The eldritch entities in the occult bookstore seemed to respond to his every thought, blurring the line between creator and creation.

In Fantasia, the symbiotic nightmares intensified their assault on Aria's sanity. The once cohesive narrative now spiraled into chaotic threads, mirroring Daniel's descent into the eldritch abyss. The eldritch symphony, now a cacophony of malevolent notes, reached a fever pitch as Aria and Daniel struggled to maintain their grasp on reality.

The symbiotic nightmares, once mere echoes of Daniel's interpretation, gained sentience. They whispered secrets of forgotten dreams, their forms evolving with each page turn. The eldritch symphony reverberating through the bookstore transcended the boundaries of imagination, entwining Daniel's waking world with Aria's nightmarish journey.

Daniel felt the weight of responsibility for the nightmares that spilled into Fantasia as he continued reading. The once passive act of interpreting the cosmic tale now felt like a dance on the edge of a reality-altering precipice. The eldritch entities in the occult bookstore seemed to respond to his every thought, blurring the line between creator and creation.

Now aware of their connection to the reader's interpretation, the symbiotic nightmares took on a sentience that mirrored Daniel's growing understanding of their influence. The eldritch entities in the occult bookstore seemed to respond to his every thought, blurring the line between creator and creation.

In Fantasia, the symbiotic nightmares intensified their assault on Aria's sanity. The once cohesive narrative now spiraled into chaotic threads, mirroring Daniel's descent into the eldritch abyss. The eldritch symphony, now a cacophony of malevolent notes, reached a fever pitch as Aria and Daniel struggled to maintain their grasp on reality.

The symbiotic nightmares, once mere echoes of Daniel's interpretation, gained sentience. They whispered secrets of forgotten dreams, their forms evolving with each page turn. The eldritch symphony reverberating through the bookstore transcended the boundaries of imagination, entwining Daniel's waking world with Aria's nightmarish journey.

As Daniel grappled with the consequences of his reading, the occult bookstore transformed into a surreal reflection of Fantasia. Eldritch entities slithered between bookshelves, and the air vibrated with the echoes of the cosmic narrative. The symbiotic connection between the reader and the protagonist became an inescapable reality, blurring the boundaries between the waking world and the dreamlands.

Now aware of their connection to the reader's interpretation, the symbiotic nightmares took on a sentience that mirrored Daniel's growing understanding of their influence. The eldritch entities in the occult bookstore seemed to respond to his every thought, blurring the line between creator and creation.

In Fantasia, the symbiotic nightmares intensified their assault on Aria's sanity. The once cohesive narrative now spiraled into chaotic threads, mirroring Daniel's descent into the eldritch abyss. The eldritch symphony, now a cacophony of malevolent notes, reached a fever pitch as Aria and Daniel struggled to maintain their grasp on reality.

The eldritch symphony reached a crescendo as the symbiotic nightmares, now unleashed upon Fantasia, roamed freely through the shattered landscapes. Their malevolent presence left echoes of chaos and fear in every corner, a testament to the unintended consequences of Daniel's reading.

As I navigated the once-serene dreamlands, the symbiotic nightmares manifested in grotesque forms, each more formidable than the last. Eldritch tendrils snaked through the air, and otherworldly whispers echoed through the distorted realms. Fantasia became a battlefield where the consequences of reading unfolded in surreal proportions.

Influenced by Daniel's interpretations, the nightmarish entities left a trail of dissonance in their wake. Trees warped into grotesque shapes, and the ground pulsated with an otherworldly heartbeat. Aria's escalating encounters with these symbiotic nightmares mirrored the intensity of the eldritch symphony, a cacophony of horror that enveloped both realms.

In the occult bookstore, the eldritch entities responded to Daniel's every thought, amplifying the roaming terrors in Fantasia. Now aware of their connection to the reader's interpretation, the symbiotic nightmares took on a sentience that mirrored Daniel's growing understanding of their influence.

As I delved deeper into "The Everlasting Nightmare," the eldritch symphony intensified, synchronizing with Aria's escalating encounters in Fantasia. The boundaries between reader and protagonist blurred further, and every turn of the page became a dance with the roaming terrors now unleashed upon both realms.

Once confined to the pages of the cosmic narrative, the nightmarish entities gained a tangible presence in the waking world. Eldritch shadows slithered through the occult bookstore, responding to the eldritch symphony with a macabre dance. Daniel's struggle to grapple with the unintended consequences of his reading mirrored Aria's descent into the ever-growing nightmare.

As Aria confronted the roaming terrors, Daniel felt the weight of responsibility for the nightmares that spilled into Fantasia. The once passive act of interpreting the cosmic tale now felt like a dance on the edge of a reality-altering precipice. The eldritch entities in the occult bookstore seemed to respond to his every thought, blurring the line between creator and creation.

The symbiotic connection between the reader and the protagonist became an inescapable reality. Fantasia and the waking world were entwined in a surreal dance of chaos and fear. The roaming terrors, born from the symbiotic nightmares, left an indelible mark on both realms, each encounter with Aria echoing through the occult bookstore.

As Aria grappled with the escalating horrors in Fantasia, Daniel struggled to maintain control over the eldritch symphony. The symbiotic nightmares, now sentient entities, responded to his every emotion, their forms evolving with each turn of the page. The occult bookstore became a battleground where the consequences of reading played out in grotesque detail.

The roaming terrors in Fantasia mirrored the eldritch entities slithering through the occult bookstore. Aria's encounters became more nightmarish, and every step she took left an imprint on the waking world. The symbiotic nightmares, driven by the cosmic disturbance, intensified their assault, creating a twisted reflection of reality in both realms.

In the occult bookstore, Daniel realized that his reading had set a cosmic dance of chaos in motion. The roaming terrors, born from the symbiotic nightmares, left a trail of horror that echoed through the eldritch symphony. The once separate narratives of reader and protagonist now converged in a macabre ballet of nightmares.

As Aria confronted the roaming terrors, Daniel felt the weight of responsibility for the nightmares that spilled into Fantasia. The once passive act of interpreting the cosmic tale now felt like a dance on the edge of a reality-altering precipice. The eldritch entities in the occult bookstore seemed to respond to his every thought, blurring the line between creator and creation.

The symbiotic connection between the reader and the protagonist became an inescapable reality. Fantasia and the waking world were entwined in a surreal dance of chaos and fear. The roaming terrors, born from the symbiotic nightmares, left an indelible mark on both realms, each encounter with Aria echoing through the occult bookstore.

As Aria grappled with the escalating horrors in Fantasia, Daniel struggled to maintain control over the eldritch symphony. The symbiotic nightmares, now sentient entities, responded to his every emotion, their forms evolving with each turn of the page. The occult bookstore became a battleground where the consequences of reading played out in grotesque detail.

The roaming terrors in Fantasia mirrored the eldritch entities slithering through the occult bookstore. Aria's encounters became more nightmarish, and every step she took left an imprint on the waking world. The symbiotic nightmares, driven by the cosmic disturbance, intensified their assault, creating a twisted reflection of reality in both realms.

In the occult bookstore, Daniel realized that his reading had set a cosmic dance of chaos in motion. The roaming terrors, born from the symbiotic nightmares, left a trail of horror that echoed through the eldritch symphony. The once separate narratives of reader and protagonist now converged in a macabre ballet of nightmares.

Chapter 7
Threads of Connection

The eldritch nightmares continued their macabre dance in Fantasia, their presence growing more palpable with every step Aria took. Unbeknownst to her, the unfolding nightmares were intricately connected to Daniel's interpretations in the waking world.

As I navigated the surreal landscapes, I felt an unseen force guiding my path, subtly steering me towards intersections with Daniel's actions. The once distinct realms of Fantasia and the waking world began to blur as if threads of connection wove them together. Every encounter with the roaming nightmares echoed with the reverberations of Daniel's reading.

Aria's path converged with Daniel's in unexpected and mysterious ways. The eldritch symphony, now a tangible force, resonated with turning pages in the occult bookstore. Each manifestation in Fantasia mirrored the evolving nightmares shaped by Daniel's interpretation. The symbiotic nightmares had become a reflection of the eldritch entities slithering through the occult bookstore.

The cosmic forces at play transcended mere coincidence. Fantasia and the occult bookstore were not separate entities. Still, they are interconnected, influencing the other in a dance orchestrated by eldritch threads. The eldritch symphony, now a harmonious blend of cosmic echoes, intensified, guiding Aria towards the heart of the narrative.

—

I could sense an unseen force at play in the dimly lit occult bookstore. Every turn of the page echoed through the eldritch symphony, resonating with Aria's footsteps in Fantasia. The connection between reader and protagonist went beyond mere coincidence; it was part of a cosmic design, a tapestry woven by eldritch threads.

The eldritch symphony intensified as the threads of connection tightened. Aria's encounters with nightmares echoed through the occult bookstore, influencing the very pages I turned. It became apparent that our fates were intertwined, each action in one realm shaping the other in a dance orchestrated by forces beyond our comprehension.

As I delved deeper into "The Everlasting Nightmare," I realized that the unseen force guiding our paths was integral to the eldritch narrative. Fantasia and the waking world were not separate but entangled, their destinies woven together by eldritch threads. Aria's struggles in the dreamlands reverberated through the occult bookstore, and the eldritch symphony responded to the unfolding cosmic design.

The synchronicity between Aria and Daniel intensified, the connection threads pulling them closer with each passing moment. Fantasia and the occult bookstore became mirrors reflecting the consequences of their actions. The eldritch nightmares, now a manifestation of the symbiotic nightmares, echoed the eldritch entities that slithered through the dimly lit aisles.

As Aria faced Eldritch's adversaries, the unseen force guided Daniel's reading, shaping the nightmares that spilled into Fantasia. The convergence of their experiences went beyond mere coincidence, revealing a cosmic design transcending the boundaries of reader and protagonist.

The connection threads tightened, and Aria and Daniel found themselves bound by a destiny forged in Eldritch's intricacies. The once separate realms now echoed with the intertwined struggles of reader and protagonist, each step in Fantasia leaving an imprint in the occult bookstore and every turning page influencing Aria's nightmarish journey.

Amid eldritch chaos, the revelation of a cosmic design unfolded. Aria and Daniel, unwittingly connected, faced the consequences of their intertwined destinies. The unseen force, a guiding hand in the eldritch narrative, orchestrated their every move, blurring the lines between the waking world and the dreamlands.

The eldritch symphony reached a crescendo as Aria and Daniel navigated the entangled realms. Fantasia and the occult bookstore became a reflection of the cosmic design, a tapestry woven with threads of connection that defied the boundaries of reality. The symbiotic nightmares, born from the convergence of their experiences, roamed freely, leaving an indelible mark on both realms.

As Aria and Daniel grappled with the revelation of their intertwined destinies, the eldritch symphony played on, echoing the cosmic design that bound them in an everlasting nightmare. Once hidden in the shadows, the threads of connection now stood revealed, guiding their every step in a dance of eldritch intricacies.

In the intricate dance of Eldritch's intricacies, Aria and Daniel were entwined in the cosmic threads, each step echoing through the intertwined destinies of Fantasia and the occult bookstore. The eldritch symphony played on, and the revelation of their connection unfolded in the ever-expanding tapestry of their nightmarish journey.

—

In the heart of Fantasia, where the veil between realms thinned, the eldritch entities manifested with a surreal grace. Their forms, ever-shifting and cosmic in nature, exuded an aura of ancient wisdom. As I stood before them, the air thick with otherworldly energy, the entities began to unravel cryptic insights into the cosmic tapestry.

The eldritch entities, harbingers of destiny, spoke in a language that transcended words, their whispers echoing through the cosmic symphony. They revealed the threads that bound me to Daniel, woven by unseen hands that manipulated the very fabric of reality. Each entity bore witness to our struggles, their cosmic eyes reflecting the interplay of destinies.

Cryptic visions unfolded before me, fragments of a grander narrative stitched together by the entities' ethereal presence. They spoke of a cosmic disturbance, an ancient force awakening from eons of slumber. My journey through Fantasia was not a chance but a carefully orchestrated dance guided by the entities as they sought to unravel the mysteries of the cosmic tapestry.

—

In the occult bookstore, shadows danced with the flickering candlelight as the eldritch symphony reached a crescendo. The turn of each page resonated with the cosmic entities' revelations in Fantasia. As I delved deeper into "The Everlasting Nightmare," the eldritch entities, weavers of destiny, stepped forth from the pages, their presence casting an otherworldly glow.

The entities' voices echoed in the dimly lit aisles, revealing the intricacies of a cosmic tale that transcended the boundaries of reader and protagonist. They spoke of destinies entwined, threads woven by their cosmic hands, pulling Aria and me closer together. The eldritch entities, ancient custodians of knowledge, shed light on the origin and purpose of the cosmic disturbance.

Intricately woven by the entities, the cosmic narrative unfolded with every revelation. Fantasia and the waking world became stages for the entities' play, and Aria and I, unwitting protagonists in their cosmic tale, navigated the intricacies of destiny. The eldritch entities' involvement hinted at a purpose beyond our understanding. This grand design compelled us to confront the ever-expanding nightmare.

The synchronicity between Aria and me intensified as the eldritch entities unveiled cryptic insights in both realms. Fantasia and the occult bookstore echoed with the cosmic revelations, each entity serving as a bridge between our realities. The threads of destiny tightened, drawing us into the cosmic narrative with an inexorable force.

Aria's encounters with the eldritch entities mirrored my own in the occult bookstore. Their cryptic revelations echoed through the eldritch symphony, vividly depicting a cosmic disturbance and a destiny entwined. The entities, weavers of fate, hinted at a purpose that transcended individual struggles, guiding us toward a revelation that would reshape the fabric of reality itself.

In the dance of cosmic revelations, Aria and I were drawn into a tapestry woven by the eldritch entities. Their cryptic insights hinted at a purpose that transcended our understanding. This cosmic tale unfolded with each turn of the page and every step in

Fantasia. The eldritch symphony played on, and the entities' revelations became the guiding threads in the ever-expanding nightmare.

–

The temporal anomalies intensified in the heart of Fantasia, where the eldritch symphony resonated through every fiber of reality. Time unraveled like an ancient tapestry subjected to cosmic forces beyond comprehension as I traversed the shattered landscapes. Moments once confined to linear progression now danced in erratic rhythms.

The temporal anomalies manifested as fleeting glimpses of forgotten epochs, jumbled and fragmented. I witnessed echoes of the past, present, and future converging in a disorienting dance. Reality wavered like a mirage, distorting the fabric of time as I struggled to maintain a semblance of order within the ever-shifting temporal currents.

In these moments of disorientation, the eldritch entities' cryptic revelations echoed louder. The threads of destiny, intricately woven by cosmic hands, now transcended space and time. Every step I took in Fantasia rippled through the temporal tapestry, leaving echoes of my presence across epochs.

—

In the occult bookstore, the temporal anomalies manifested as flickering candles casting shadows that danced out of sync with the rhythmic pulsations of the eldritch symphony. As I read deeper into "The Everlasting Nightmare," the boundaries between Fantasia and the waking world blurred, creating a surreal and unpredictable cosmic landscape.

The temporal fabric of reality shattered, intertwining Fantasia and the waking world in unprecedented ways. I felt the disorienting effects of fragmented realities colliding, each page turned, opening a portal between temporal states. The dimly lit aisles transformed into a nexus where past, present, and future coexist in a harmonious discord.

In this cosmic dance of shattered realities, the occult bookstore became a focal point where temporal threads crossed and converged. The eldritch entities' revelations guided me through the labyrinth of time, unveiling the intricate connections between Aria's journey and my exploration of the cosmic narrative.

As Aria and I navigated the intensifying temporal anomalies, the symbiotic connection between our experiences deepened. Fantasia and the occult bookstore echoed with the resonance of fractured time, each anomaly drawing us closer together. The blurred boundaries between temporal states became the stage for our intertwined destinies.

The shattered realities created a cosmic tapestry where Aria's steps in Fantasia echoed in the waking world, and my exploration of the cosmic narrative left imprints on the temporal currents. In this dance of temporal distortions, the eldritch entities' revelations served as a guide, unraveling the mysteries of the ever-expanding nightmare across the intricate threads of time.

Chapter 8
Dance of Nightmares

In the twisted landscapes of Fantasia, a formidable symbiotic nightmare emerged from the cosmic tapestry, a manifestation born from the depths of Daniel's interpretations. The eldritch menace, a grotesque amalgamation of Eldritch horror and Daniel's waking world fears stood before me like a nightmare.

Its form was ever-shifting, a surreal collage of tendrils that echoed the shadows of the occult bookstore, spectral whispers that mirrored the flickering candles, and a darkness that mirrored Daniel's deepest apprehensions. The symbiotic nightmare was a cosmic mirror, reflecting the intertwined dance of our realities.

As I confronted this eldritch embodiment, its presence resonated with the symphony that permeated Fantasia. It was a living echo of the eldritch forces that responded to the cosmic narrative. In its form, I saw the blurred lines between reader and protagonist, observer and participant in the unfolding nightmare.

The nightmare's tendrils reached out, entwining with the very essence of Fantasia. Shadows danced in macabre unison, echoing the eldritch symphony's unsettling melody. Aria's senses were assaulted by a cacophony of eldritch whispers, each voice a fragment of Daniel's readings, each word a brushstroke in the painting of cosmic terror.

The confrontation unfolded as a harrowing dance in the heart of Fantasia. Aria, determined and resolute, faced the symbiotic nightmare with courage forged in the crucible of cosmic disturbances. With each movement, the nightmare adapted, weaving through the threads of Eldritch horror and Daniel's fears with eerie precision.

Aria's struggle against the nightmare became a desperate battle, the stakes escalating with every passing moment. The nightmare's male whispers echoed Daniel's deepest fears, amplifying the cosmic terror gripping Fantasia. Aria's every effort to overcome the eldritch adversary pushed her to the limits of her abilities.

In this cosmic dance, Aria's valiant attempts to subdue the nightmare mirrored Daniel's reading in the waking world. Every emotion, twist, and turn resonated through the symbiotic connection, creating a surreal tapestry where the reader and protagonist were bound inextricably by the eldritch threads of the ever-expanding nightmare.

The nightmare's form, an embodiment of cosmic horror, shifted with the ebb and flow of the eldritch symphony. Aria's movements were met with an unsettling counter as if the nightmare anticipated her every action. Shadows clung to her like ethereal chains, each step forward echoing through the vast expanse of Fantasia.

The cosmic dance intensified, a whirlwind of eldritch energies and Aria's indomitable spirit colliding in a crescendo of surreal chaos. As she grappled with the nightmare, the boundary between Fantasia and the waking world blurred even further, and the consequences of this metaphysical clash rippled through the fabric of both realms.

Aria's determination became a beacon, a singular resistance point against the encroaching nightmares. Yet, with each passing moment, the eldritch adversary grew more muscular, feeding on the cosmic energy woven into the very fabric of Fantasia. The struggle was not just against a tangible foe but an existential battle against the unraveling of realities.

As the dance of nightmares reached its zenith, Aria's vision blurred between the eldritch nightmare and the words that Daniel read in the waking world. The symbiotic connection intensified, pushing both Aria and Daniel to the brink of madness. The boundary between reader and protagonist, observer and participant, dissolved in the maddening embrace of cosmic horror.

—

In the waking world, my challenges mirrored Aria's otherworldly confrontation with an eerie synchronicity that defied conventional explanation. The mundane and the cosmic became interwoven threads in the grand tapestry of the Everlasting Nightmare, creating a perplexing dance that transcended the boundaries of reality.

As I navigated the waking world challenge, the city streets seemed to pulse with eldritch energy, responding to the cosmic symphony from Fantasia. Shadows twisted and contorted, taking on shapes reminiscent of the eldritch nightmares that plagued Aria's journey. Every step I took resonated with the intricate choreography of the dance, a cosmic ballet of nightmares that unfolded both in the waking world and the realms beyond.

The waking world challenge was an uncanny reflection of Aria's Eldritch confrontation. Each trial presented me with echoes of the cosmic struggles in Fantasia as if the boundaries between realities were merely illusions ready to be shattered. It was more than a mere parallel; it was a convergence, a dance where every movement in one reality rippled through the fabric of the other.

As the waking world challenge intensified, the blurring of boundaries between realities became increasingly profound. The city, once a backdrop to my waking life, transformed into a surreal landscape, mirroring the shattered landscapes of Fantasia. Buildings stretched and contorted, and the air crackled with the same cosmic tension that defined Aria's journey.

The uncanny resemblance between the waking world challenge and Aria's Eldritch confrontation went beyond mere coincidence. It was a manifestation of the symbiotic connection that bound our fates, a realization that shook the foundations of my understanding. Every decision I made in the waking world had consequences that reverberated through the cosmic tapestry, shaping the very fabric of Fantasia.

As I faced each waking world obstacle, it became evident that the challenges were intricately linked to Aria's cosmic journey. The dance of nightmares wasn't confined to Fantasia alone; it spilled over into the waking world, creating a dance floor where the boundaries between realms dissolved. The waking world challenge wasn't just a reflection but a tangible manifestation of the cosmic design that bound Aria and me inextricably to the Everlasting Nightmare.

The stakes escalated as the dual realities converged, blurring the lines between reader and protagonist, observer and participant. The waking world challenge, once a mirror, now held its own weight in the cosmic ballet—a testament to the intricate dance of nightmares that unfolded across realms, each step resonating with the ever-expanding nightmare that entwined our destinies.

—

As I navigated the ever-shifting landscapes of Fantasia, the boundary between reality and fantasy continued to blur, each step resonating with the dance of nightmares that unfolded across the realms. The connection intensified, threading itself through every aspect of my existence. The waking world challenges Daniel faced echoed through the cosmic narrative, seamlessly integrating into the eldritch tapestry that defined our intertwined destinies.

The once-clear lines between the waking world and Fantasia began to fade, replaced by a seamless integration of challenges that defied the conventional order of things. Each trial Daniel confronted resonated with an eerie familiarity in Fantasia as if the waking world had become a stage for the cosmic ballet of nightmares.

Reality and fantasy collided with a force that shook the very foundations of both realms. The waking world's challenges, once confined to the city's concrete jungles, now spilled into Fantasia's surreal landscapes. The cosmic narrative, in turn, bled into the waking world, creating a tapestry where the boundaries between the realms were nothing more than threads waiting to be unraveled.

—

The dance of nightmares reached a crescendo as Fantasia's nightmarish elements began to bleed into the waking world. The city streets, once familiar, now bore the surreal imprint of cosmic malevolence. Shadows stretched and contorted, mimicking the eldritch entities that roamed Fantasia's shattered landscapes. The barriers between realms crumbled, and the once-distinct boundaries dissolved into an indistinguishable blur.

As I faced waking world challenges, the influence of Fantasia's nightmares became palpable. Each trial brought echoes of cosmic malevolence, an undeniable intertwining of destinies that transcended the limitations of reality. Once confined to the pages of "The Everlasting Nightmare," the eldritch manifestations" now walked the waking world, leaving an indelible mark on the city's fabric.

The surreal ballet of nightmares unfolded with a relentless rhythm, where the lines between reality and fantasy became illusions. Every encounter and challenge was a testament to the unraveling of boundaries that held the waking world and Fantasia in separate spheres. The veil between realms thinned, revealing a cosmic tapestry where Aria's journey and my waking world struggles were threads intricately woven into a grand design.

The dance of nightmares had become a seamless ballet, where the distinction between reality and fantasy lost meaning. As Aria and I faced the escalating challenges, it became evident that our destinies were no longer bound by the limitations of individual realms but were threads woven into the very fabric of the Everlasting Nightmare.

Chapter 9
The Eldritch Symphony

The ethereal dance continued, drawing more performers onto the cosmic stage. Nyctalus, the spectral guide who had first ushered me into Fantasia, was now accompanied by new Eldritch allies. Each one, with an aura of ancient wisdom and mysterious purpose, seamlessly blended into the ever-evolving narrative that entwined my destiny with Daniel's. Their spectral forms resonated with the cosmic energy, their very presence echoing through the realms.

Among these enigmatic allies was Luminae, a shimmering entity whose light cast away shadows, revealing glimpses of hidden truths. Her radiance, a counterpoint to the looming darkness, hinted at the delicate balance required in the cosmic ballet. Another ally, Umbra, wielded the shadows with an artistry that mirrored the enigmatic depths of the Everlasting Nightmare. Each Eldritch ally brought a unique essence to the cosmic symphony, enriching the narrative with their abilities and knowledge.

As we ventured deeper into the cosmic labyrinth, their cryptic whispers became a guiding melody, directing us toward the heart of the Everlasting Nightmare. Luminae's light illuminated the obscured paths, while Umbra's shadows concealed us from the prying eyes of malevolent forces. Like notes in a celestial composition, the Eldritch allies played their parts in the intricate dance that unfolded across Fantasia and the waking world.

—

While Eldritch allies joined our cosmic ballet, the malevolent entities from the cosmic Abyss intensified their presence. Their emergence was not merely a challenge but a revelation of the dark undercurrents courting through the Everlasting Nightmare. Each adversary, born from the unfathomable depths of cosmic horror, added dissonance to the symphony, their malevolent notes clashing with the harmonious whispers of our spectral guides.

Among these adversaries, the Shrouded Harbinger embodied a nightmarish force that distorted reality. Its presence rippled through Fantasia and the waking world, leaving chaos. Another, known as the Abyssal Seraph, manifested as a winged creature with eyes that held the weight of forgotten eons. These entities, drawn by the cosmic disturbance, became formidable challenges, testing our mettle and reshaping the narrative with every confrontation.

As we faced these cosmic adversaries, the complexities of the Everlasting Nightmare's design became clearer. The Eldritch Symphony, once a melodic dance, now echoed with the cacophony of discordant forces. Our journey, now fraught with peril, demanded our resilience and a deeper understanding of our cosmic roles.

The dance of nightmares expanded into an epic symphony, where Eldritch allies and adversaries engaged in a cosmic dialogue. Fantasia and the waking world were the stages, and the fate of both realms hung in the balance as the cosmic symphony approached its climactic movement.

—

Amid our cosmic journey, a profound connection between Daniel and me unfolded, transcending the boundaries of Fantasia and the waking world. Like ethereal threads, shared visions wove a tapestry of our intertwined destinies. As I navigated the surreal landscapes of Fantasia, Daniel glimpsed my challenges and triumphs through the shared visions that danced in his waking world.

During one such vision, as I confronted the Shrouded Harbinger, Daniel bore witness to the cosmic struggle, feeling the weight of each blow and the surge of eldritch energies. The shared experience blurred the lines between reader and protagonist, observer and participant, creating a symbiotic link that transcended the confines of the Everlasting Nightmare.

The visions became a manifestation of the cosmic threads binding our fates together. Every step I took resonated in Daniel's reality, and his reactions echoed in the fantastical realm. It was as if the fabric of the cosmic tapestry responded to our shared journey, acknowledging the intricate dance we performed across realms.

Like enigmatic chapters in the cosmic narrative, the shared visions began to reveal glimpses of a grander design at play. As I delved deeper into "The Everlasting Nightmare," the revelations echoed in the waking world, forming a bridge connecting reality and fantasy realms. Aria's struggles against the Abyssal Seraph, her encounters with Eldritch allies, and the cosmic disturbances resonated through the shared visions.

Aria and I stood at the threshold of a celestial gate in one profound vision, its arcane symbols intertwining with cosmic energies. The gate, a metaphorical doorway between our realities, hinted at a purpose beyond our understanding. The cosmic design seemed orchestrated by forces older than time, and our roles in this intricate dance became more apparent with each shared vision.

Aria and I realized that our destinies were not mere products of chance as the cosmic tapestry unraveled before us. We were players in a cosmic drama scripted by eldritch forces, each twist and turn a deliberate choreography designed to test the boundaries of reality and fantasy.

The shared visions, a manifestation of the more excellent cosmic design, became guideposts illuminating our path through the labyrinthine narrative of the Everlasting Nightmare. Our destinies, now intricately entwined, unfolded like an ancient scroll revealing secrets that transcended the limitations of mortal comprehension. The cosmic tapestry awaited its next unfurling, and Aria and I were. Still, instruments play our parts in the grand symphony of eldritch existence.

—

The Everlasting Nightmare took an ominous turn as the symbiotic nightmares, once born from the convergence of Daniel's interpretations and Fantasia's reality, underwent a profound metamorphosis. They evolved into nightmarish symphonies, each contributing to a cosmic harmony resonating through the Dreamlands.

As I traversed the shattered landscapes, the air pulsed with eldritch resonance. Once chaotic and disjointed, the nightmarish symphonies now melded into a terrifying harmony, creating a dissonant melody that echoed the disturbance in the Dreamlands. The entities moved with an eerie synchronicity, like players in a malevolent orchestra, contributing to the cosmic dissonance that permeated every corner of Fantasia.

–

In the waking world, the discordant melodies of the Abyss manifested as haunting echoes that reverberated through the air. The once subtle connection between my readings and the cosmic narrative became more palpable. The nightmarish symphonies transcended the boundaries of Fantasia, their presence manifesting in the waking world as well.

As I explored the occult depths of "The Everlasting Nightmare," the discordant melodies became the backdrop to my waking reality. Shadows danced in rhythm to the dissonance, and eldritch whispers seeped through the veil between worlds. Now intertwined in unprecedented ways, the waking world and Fantasia echoed the evolving cosmic symphony.

Aria and I, bound by the cosmic threads, were compelled to navigate the surreal landscapes shaped by the evolving dissonance. Each step in Fantasia echoed in the waking world, and every revelation from

"The Everlasting Nightmare" resonated through the cosmic tapestry, blurring the lines between reality and fantasy.

The discordant crescendo marked a turning point in our journey. As Aria confronted the nightmarish symphonies in Fantasia, I grappled with their echoes in the waking world. The eldritch melodies intensified, compelling us to confront the malevolent forces that sought to disrupt the fragile balance between realms. The dance of nightmares, now transformed into a cosmic symphony, hinted at a crescendo of cosmic proportions. Aria and I stood at the center of this dissonant storm.

Chapter 10
Veil of Madness

The Everlasting Nightmare plunged Aria into a realm of unprecedented challenges. The symbiotic connection between us reached a critical juncture, its intensity pushing us to the brink of our mental and emotional limits. Once a canvas of surreal wonders, Fantasia has transformed into a crucible of cosmic trials.

As I confronted the nightmarish symphonies, their discordant melodies reverberated through every fiber of my being. The symbiotic nightmares, born from the intertwining of Daniel's interpretations and Fantasia's reality, grew more formidable. Each encounter tested the strength of our connection, amplifying the cosmic forces that bound us together.

The veil between realms trembled in the waking world, and the unseen forces that shaped our intertwined destinies manifested unsettlingly. Aria and I faced challenges that transcended the boundaries of our understanding. The intensification of symbiotic nightmares and cosmic disturbances tested the resilience of both protagonists.

The occult depths of "The Everlasting Nightmare" mirrored our challenges in Fantasia. Every revelation within the eldritch tome seemed to amplify the cosmic dissonance, creating a feedback loop that pushed us further into the realms of the unknown. The struggle against unseen forces became a battle not just for survival but for the very fabric of our sanity.

Aria and I found ourselves entangled in a dance with madness as the symbiotic connection reached its zenith. The veil of sanity wavered, revealing glimpses of eldritch truths that threatened to unravel the fragile tapestry of our minds. The cosmic forces, relentless and enigmatic, pushed us beyond the limits of human understanding, and the line between protagonist and reader, observer and participant, blurred in the dissonant symphony of The Everlasting Nightmare.

—

As the nightmarish symphonies crescendoed, the cryptic insights from the Eldritch allies became both a beacon and a maze within Fantasia's shifting landscapes. Nyctalus, in spectral form, guided me through surreal dimensions, revealing fragmented glimpses of the cosmic narrative. His words echoed like distant whispers, resonating with the harmonies of the ever-evolving nightmare.

With each revelation, I immersed myself in a dance with the unknown. The guardians of secrets unfolded layers of the disturbance, teasing the threads that wove through my destiny. Yet, their insights remained veiled in a cosmic language, challenging my comprehension and beckoning me to embrace the enigma.

–

In the tangible world, the eldritch ink on the pages of "The Everlasting Nightmare" mirrored the guardians' ethereal messages. The script, a complex dance of symbols and runes, revealed their role as protectors and the intricate connections between Fantasia and reality. I traced the patterns, hoping to decipher the cosmic symphony reverberating through the pages.

The Eldritch allies became guardians of the veil, holding the delicate balance between our realms. Each revelation in the eldritch script hinted at a cosmic choreography, where every step Aria and I took resonated with the unfolding narrative. The guardians' guidance transformed the act of reading into a ritual, a communion with forces beyond human understanding.

As Aria and I embraced the cryptic visions, the boundaries between the reader and the protagonist blurred further. The cosmic dance led us deeper into the labyrinth of intertwined destinies, where echoes within the cosmic tapestry hinted at an impending revelation. This revelation could illuminate the path forward or plunge us further into the veiled depths of the Eldritch nightmare.

—

The trembling veil between Fantasia and the waking world climaxed, merging the realms into a surreal amalgamation. As I traversed the fragmented landscapes, every step echoed through both realities. The symbiotic connection with Daniel intensified, weaving our destinies into a complex tapestry of shared experiences.

The cosmic forces binding us grew more robust, revealing the interconnected madness within. It wasn't just the eldritch nightmares that haunted our footsteps; it was the unraveling of our perceptions, plunging us into the depths of a shared, fractured reality. The line between Aria and Daniel blurred as the veil thinned, and our minds intertwined in a dance of cosmic chaos.

—

The unraveling madness mirrored the eldritch script in "The Everlasting Nightmare." Each turn of the page etched more profoundly into the cosmic narrative, pulling Aria and me into a shared descent. The abyss within ourselves mirrored the abyss in Fantasia and the boundaries between waking and dreaming shattered like fragile glass.

As the cosmic forces bared our hidden truths, sanity hung by a fragile thread. The symbiotic fusion revealed the nightmares born from our fears and the resilience within us. Confronting the madness became a dual journey, where every revelation in the waking world mirrored Aria's struggles in Fantasia and vice versa. The cosmic ballet orchestrated a dance of revelation and introspection, pushing us to confront the abyss within and navigate the fragile terrain between reason and the unknown.

The symbiotic connection, once a cosmic thread linking Aria and me, now emerged as a force that plunged us into a shared descent. As the veil between realities trembled, we faced the profound challenge of navigating the thin line between sanity and madness, caught in the grip of the cosmic forces that sought to reshape our understanding of reality.

Chapter 11
Threads Unravel

The cosmic tapestry, once a beautiful dance of interconnected destinies, now bore the ominous touch of the Weaver of Nightmares. As I traversed the fragmented landscapes of Fantasia, a palpable malevolence lingered in the air. The eldritch disturbance intensified, and with it, my awareness of the sinister force that wove nightmares into the very fabric of this realm.

The Weaver's influence surpassed the mere manipulation of dreams; a pervasive malevolence reached the core of Fantasia itself. Shadows slithered across shattered landscapes, each echo foreshadowing the Weaver's looming presence. Every step I took was accompanied by an unsettling sense of being watched, as if Weaver's unseen eyes bore into the essence of my existence.

—

As the pages turned in "The Everlasting Nightmare," the echoes of Aria's encounters with shadows reverberated through my waking world. The malevolent force that shaped Fantasia extended its tendrils beyond the cosmic narrative, casting shadows that echoed into my reality. Whispers of the Weaver's influence manifested in the subtle shifts of shadows, a prelude to the impending cosmic storm.

The tension grew every moment, mirroring Aria's awareness of the Weaver's watchful gaze. The malevolence that seeped through the veiled boundaries between Fantasia and the waking world hinted at a looming confrontation. The threads of destiny, once intricately woven, now unraveled under the ominous influence of the Weaver of Nightmares, setting the stage for a cosmic battle that transcended the realms of dream and reality.

—

The Weaver's influence manifested with an unsettling intensity, distorting Fantasia's very fabric of dreams. The once-vivid dreams unraveled into nightmarish tableaus as I traversed the surreal landscapes. The skies twisted into surreal hues, and the ground beneath my feet morphed into an ever-shifting mosaic of distorted reality.

The Weaver's malevolence reached the core of Fantasia, manipulating dreams into surreal landscapes of cosmic horror. Each step I took echoed with the distorted whispers of the dreamers whose fantasies had been twisted into nightmares. The Weaver's dark touch was undeniable, and the threads connecting me to this cosmic tapestry grew more intricate, binding my fate with Daniel's in ways I couldn't comprehend.

—

In the waking world, the malevolence of the Weaver began to cast its shadow over my reality. The dreams I once dismissed as mere figments of imagination now revealed themselves as threads woven by the sinister architect. The Weaver's influence transcended the boundaries between Fantasia and reality. It intertwines Aria and me in a cosmic dance scripted by its dark design.

Revelations unfolded within "The Everlasting Nightmare," exposing the intricacies of the cosmic threads the Weaver manipulated. Every turn of the page unveiled the Weaver's role as a malevolent force shaping destinies. The realization dawned that Aria and I were entangled in a narrative woven by the

Weaver. As the cosmic threads tightened, the boundaries between our separate realities blurred into a tapestry of intertwined fates.

—

In the ever-expanding tapestry of cosmic horror, the insidious influence of the Weaver reached new depths, distorting the fabric of dreams across realms. Fantasia, once a sanctuary of fantastical landscapes, now echoed with nightmarish visions orchestrated by the malevolent force. As the Weaver's presence intensified, the once-clear boundaries between Fantasia and the waking world crumbled like ancient ruins, leaving only a disorienting landscape of interconnected nightmares.

Daniel found himself ensnared in waking world challenges that mirrored my struggles within Fantasia. The surreal landscapes, born from the nightmares spun by the Weaver, materialized in the waking world, blurring the lines between reality and the cosmic narrative. The streets pulsated with eldritch energy, buildings morphing into grotesque structures reminiscent of the nightmares Aria faced in Fantasia. The city seemed to breathe with an otherworldly life, resonating with the cosmic discord reverberating through the waking world and beyond.

—

As I ventured deeper into the waking world, it became evident that the nightmares weren't confined to Fantasia alone. The challenges I encountered closely resemble Aria's struggles against the malevolent force within the dream realms. The cityscape transformed into a nightmarish reflection of the cosmic discord that echoed in Fantasia, blurring the boundaries between waking reality and the surreal landscapes of the Weaver's nightmares.

With every shared challenge, the connection between Aria and me grew more intricate, intertwining our destinies in a cosmic dance. The nightmares, once disparate, now converged in a symphony of shared fears, echoing the dissonant melody of the Weaver's malevolence. The Weaver's influence transcended the dream realms, leaving a palpable sense of unease that permeated every corner of the waking world.

As we faced challenges that mirrored each other's struggles, the symbiotic connection between Aria and me reached a critical juncture. The nightmares became a reflection of our shared journey, revealing hidden truths that lay buried beneath the layers of cosmic horror. The boundaries between waking reality and Fantasia continued to erode, and the cosmic tapestry, woven by the malevolent force, tightened its grip on our intertwined fates.

Chapter 12
Nightmares in Tandem

The air in Fantasia crackled with oppressive energy as I ventured deeper into the surreal landscapes woven by the Weaver of Nightmares. The malevolent force, once a distant architect of cosmic discord, now manifested directly before me. The very essence of the Weaver permeated the distorted realms, and every step I took felt like a dance with the shadows of impending despair.

I confronted the Weaver's sinister presence in the heart of Fantasia, where reality and nightmare converged. Its form, a shifting silhouette of darkness, exuded an aura of ancient malevolence. Eyes devoid of empathy met mine, sending shivers down my spine. The distorted landscapes twisted and contorted in response to Weaver's will, creating an otherworldly stage for our confrontation.

The Weaver spoke through the echo of its voice, a chorus of whispers that resonated in the air. "Aria Evernight," it intoned, the words carrying the weight of eons. "You traverse the tapestry of existence, yet you are blind to the threads that weave your destiny. Embrace the nightmares, for within them lies the revelation you seek."

My inner turmoil echoed in the surreal surroundings as I grappled with the Weaver's cryptic words. Each step forward was met with resistance, the fabric of Fantasia resisting my intrusion into its cosmic secrets. As the malevolent force intensified its presence, the shadows of despair coalesced into nightmarish entities, each mirroring the struggles within my own soul.

While Aria faced the Weaver's direct and chilling encounters in Fantasia, the waking world mirrored the escalating tension. Shadows danced across the cityscape, each harbinger of despair, echoing Aria's struggles against the malevolent force. The boundaries between Fantasia and reality continued to blur, creating an unnerving synchronization of nightmares.

In the waking world, the buildings cast elongated shadows that seemed to reach out, mirroring the Weaver's influence in Fantasia. As I navigated the distorted streets, the shadows morphed into grotesque figures, mirroring the malevolence that Aria confronted within the cosmic tapestry. Every step became a battle against the encroaching darkness, a struggle to maintain sanity amidst the discordant symphony of nightmares.

Once familiar, the streets twisted and contorted with the same surreal distortion gripping Fantasia. Faces in the crowds became distorted reflections of the malevolent force that pervaded both realms. It was as if the nightmares had transcended the cosmic boundaries, entwining the waking world in the same dance of shadows Aria faced within Fantasia.

–

The Weaver's shadows, once mere echoes, now coalesced into tangible adversaries, testing the limits of my resolve. Each confrontation was a dance with despair, a struggle to retain my sanity in the face of the malevolent force. The distorted landscapes twisted and writhed, responding to the Weaver's sinister will, creating an ever-shifting battleground.

With every encounter, the Weaver's influence seeped deeper into Fantasia, leaving a trail of cosmic dissonance. The shadows, extensions of the Weaver's malevolence, became more formidable, pushing me to despair. Yet, within the dance of shadows, a spark of defiance ignited. The more I confronted the Weaver, the more I glimpsed the hidden threads that bound our fates together, unveiling the cosmic design at play.

The very essence of Fantasia seemed to pulse with the Weaver's malevolence. This cosmic heartbeat resonated with every step I took. It was as if the nightmares had become a symphony, each discordant note echoing the struggles within my soul. The surreal landscapes transformed into a surreal stage, and I, the reluctant protagonist, danced amidst the shadows of cosmic dissonance.

—

As Aria confronted the Weaver in Fantasia, the waking world echoed the cosmic ballet. The distorted shadows in the city took on a rhythmic dance, mirroring the surreal landscapes that Aria navigated. Faces in the crowds seemed to move synchronously with the cosmic heartbeat, their expressions reflecting the hidden struggles within Fantasia.

The nightmares that haunted Aria transcended the boundaries of realms, seeping into the waking world like an ethereal mist. The streets became a stage for the cosmic ballet, and I, an unwitting participant, moved to the rhythm of the discordant symphony. The line between observer and participant blurred as the cosmic forces entwined our destinies in an intricate dance of shadows.

The city became a canvas for the malevolent force, its influence shaping the very fabric of reality. Buildings contorted with the same surreal distortion that gripped Fantasia, and the boundaries between waking and dreaming became elusive. The Weaver's influence transcended the cosmic boundaries, seamlessly integrating nightmares that echoed between realms.

–

A realization dawned in the heart of the surreal stage, where shadows danced and nightmares converged. The cosmic threads binding me to the Weaver were not chains of submission but threads of resilience. With each confrontation, I embraced the nightmares, understanding that the key to unraveling the cosmic tapestry lay within their discordant symphony.

The dance with shadows became a dance of self-discovery, a journey through the echoes of despair that revealed the strength within. As the malevolent force intensified, I stood resilient, a beacon of defiance amidst the cosmic dissonance. Once adversaries, the nightmares became stepping stones toward understanding the more excellent cosmic design.

—

In the waking world, as the city pulsated with the rhythm of the cosmic ballet, I felt the unseen threads weaving through my existence. The nightmares that mirrored Aria's struggles became a reflection of the interconnected cosmic tapestry. Every challenge, every distorted shadow, was a thread that bound us together in a dance of nightmares that transcended both realms.

The line between waking and dreaming blurred further as the cosmic forces intensified their influence. The challenges I faced mirrored Aria's confrontations with the Weaver, and with each mirrored struggle, the unseen threads tightened. The cosmic design at play revealed itself in glimpses, cryptic insights that hinted at a purpose beyond our understanding.

As the dance of shadows unfolded, the boundaries between Fantasia and the waking world became indistinguishable. The nightmares, once confined to the realm of dreams, now bled into reality, creating a surreal landscape where the cosmic threads intertwined. The Weaver's influence, once confined to Fantasia, now reached across realms, entwining our destinies in a symphony of cosmic design.

–

With every step in the dance of shadows, I embraced the nightmares as stepping stones toward unraveling the cosmic tapestry. The malevolent force sought to break my spirit, but a melody of defiance resonated within the echoes of despair. The distorted landscapes, the shadows that morphed and twisted, became a canvas for the resilience within.

The Weaver's cryptic whispers continued to echo, but they became a source of empowerment instead of submission. Each confrontation with the malevolent force strengthened my resolve, revealing the hidden threads of resilience woven into the fabric of Fantasia. Once a tumultuous symphony, the cosmic ballet now resonated with the echoes of defiance.

—

In the waking world, the dance of shadows mirrored Aria's struggles within Fantasia. Every challenge became a thread woven into the cosmic tapestry, binding our destinies in ways that transcended understanding. The nightmares, once confined to the realm of dreams, now shaped the waking world, creating a surreal fusion of reality and fantasy.

As the cosmic forces intensified, the unseen threads tightened, drawing Aria and me closer to the heart of the disturbance. The challenges mirrored each other, creating a seamless integration of nightmares that echoed between realms. The Weaver's influence, once confined to Fantasia, now extended its malevolence into the waking world, entwining our destinies in a symphony of cosmic design.

–

In the heart of the surreal stage, as Aria and I confronted the malevolent force, the nightmares converged into a symphony of cosmic design. The dance of shadows, once a chaotic discord, now resonated with a harmony born from the resilience within. The unseen threads tightened, drawing us closer to the heart of the disturbance, where the Weaver's influence reached across realms.

As Aria and I faced the malevolent force, the boundaries between Fantasia and the waking world dissolved. The nightmares, once confined to dreams, now bled into reality, shaping a surreal landscape where the cosmic tapestry unfolded. The Weaver's cryptic whispers became a guide, revealing insights into the grander narrative at play.

With every step in the dance of shadows, Aria and I moved towards the convergence of nightmares, where the cosmic forces entwined our destinies in a symphony of cosmic design. The malevolent force sought to break our spirits, but we found a melody of defiance within the echoes of despair. The cosmic ballet, once a tumultuous symphony, now became a harmonious convergence of nightmares, revealing the hidden threads that bound our fates together in the ever-unfolding tapestry of "The Everlasting Nightmare."

—

In the heart of Fantasia, the nightmares underwent a sinister metamorphosis. The once chaotic and primal dreams evolved into intricate and insidious scenarios, each a testament to the Weaver's dark artistry. As I ventured deeper into the cosmic labyrinth, the distorted dreamscapes mirrored the complexity of the malevolent force that sought to unravel the fabric of existence.

The surreal landscapes twisted and contorted, responding to the Weaver's will with an unsettling grace. Every step I took led me through scenarios that defied logic and sanity. The nightmares, once mere manifestations of cosmic discord, now became intricate puzzles, testing my resolve and the fabric of my understanding.

The distorted dreamscapes echoed with the Weaver's cryptic whispers, each scenario a canvas for the malevolent force's intricate design. Shadows danced with purpose, and the air pulsed with an otherworldly rhythm. The challenges unfolded were not random manifestations but carefully crafted visions, each step a calculated dance with nightmarish intricacy.

—

In the waking world, the cityscape transformed into a reflection of the cosmic labyrinth Aria navigated within Fantasia. Buildings contorted with the same surreal distortion, and the shadows cast intricate patterns on the streets. The malevolent force's dark artistry extended beyond the cosmic boundaries, creating a seamless integration of nightmares between realms.

As I moved through the waking world, the scenarios mirrored the visions Aria faced within the Weaver's labyrinth. The nightmares were no longer primal and chaotic but carefully crafted visions of cosmic horror. Each street and building became a canvas for the malevolent force's intricate design, reflecting the dark artistry of Weaver's influence.

The city became a stage for the dance with nightmarish intricacy. Faces in the crowds morphed into grotesque masks, each expression reflecting the cosmic horror unfolding within Fantasia. Every step I took resonated with the rhythm of the distorted dreamscapes, a surreal ballet that transcended the boundaries between waking and dreaming.

In the heart of the cosmic labyrinth, where nightmares unfolded with intricate precision, I navigated the distorted dreamscapes with a growing sense of urgency. The challenges mirrored the malevolent force's dark artistry, each scenario carefully crafted to test my resolve and sanity. The air pulsated with the rhythmic echoes of the Weaver's design, and every step became a dance with nightmarish intricacy.

The surreal landscapes twisted and contorted, responding to the malevolent force's will with an unsettling grace. Shadows took on intricate forms, dancing with purpose as they wove a tapestry of cosmic horror. The distorted dreamscapes were no longer random manifestations. Still, they calculated visions that sought to unravel the very fabric of my understanding.

As I faced each scenario, the Weaver's cryptic whispers guided me through the intricacies of its design. Every challenge unfolded deliberately, revealing the malevolent force's mastery over the cosmic tapestry. Once chaotic, the nightmares became a symphony of intricate horrors, each step a calculated dance with the Weaver's dark artistry.

—

In the waking world, the city echoed with the intricate patterns of the cosmic labyrinth. Buildings twisted and contorted with the same surreal distortion that gripped Fantasia. Shadows danced on the streets, each movement reflecting the malevolent force's dark artistry. The nightmares were no longer random disturbances but carefully crafted visions that mirrored the Weaver's influence.

As I moved through the distorted cityscape, the dance with nightmarish intricacy unfolded with each step. Faces in the crowds became masks of cosmic horror, their expressions reflecting the malevolent force's design. The city became a canvas for Weaver's dark artistry, a surreal stage where the boundaries between waking and dreaming blurred.

The scenarios I faced mirrored Aria's challenges within Fantasia, each step resonating with the rhythmic echoes of the distorted dreamscapes. The nightmares, once primal, now unfolded with a deliberate elegance, revealing the intricate patterns of the malevolent force's design. The dance with nightmarish intricacy became a surreal ballet that transcended the boundaries between realms.

—

As I moved through Weaver's labyrinth, the nightmares became threads of complexity, weaving through the very fabric of Fantasia. Each scenario unfolded with a calculated elegance, testing my resilience and the limits of cosmic understanding. The distorted dreamscapes, once a chaotic tapestry, now revealed the intricate patterns that bound me to the malevolent force.

With every step, the cryptic whispers guided me through the complexities of the Weaver's design. Shadows danced with purpose, and the air pulsed with an otherworldly rhythm. My challenges were not mere obstacles but threads that bound me to the cosmic tapestry. The dance with nightmarish intricacy became a journey through the hidden layers of the malevolent force's influence.

—

In the waking world, the dance with nightmarish intricacy mirrored Aria's journey within Fantasia. The distorted cityscape became a canvas for the malevolent force's intricate design, each step unraveling threads that bound me to the cosmic tapestry. The nightmares, once primal, now unfolded with a calculated elegance that echoed the Weaver's influence.

As I faced each scenario, the echoes of the cosmic ballet resonated with the rhythm of the distorted dreamscapes. The intricacies of the malevolent force's design became more apparent with every step, revealing the threads that bound my destiny to Aria's. The dance with nightmarish intricacy transcended the boundaries between waking and dreaming, creating a surreal fusion of reality and fantasy.

—

Aria and I moved through the distorted dreamscapes in the heart of the cosmic labyrinth, each step dancing with nightmarish intricacy. The malevolent force's dark artistry unfolded with calculated precision, testing our resilience and understanding of the cosmic tapestry. The nightmares, once chaotic, now became threads of complexity that bound us to the Weaver's influence.

As Aria and I navigated through the surreal landscapes, the boundaries between Fantasia and the waking world blurred. The intricate patterns of the malevolent force's design extended seamlessly between realms, creating a convergence of nightmares that echoed between waking and dreaming. The dance with nightmarish intricacy became a surreal ballet, revealing the hidden threads that entwined our destinies in the cosmic tapestry of "The Everlasting Nightmare."

The distorted cityscape continued to reflect the intricate nightmares within Fantasia, each building and street a canvas for the malevolent force's design. As I moved through the waking world, the challenges intensified, aligning seamlessly with the nightmares crafted by the Weaver.

The boundaries between the realms blurred further, and the waking world echoed the cosmic discord that unfolded within Fantasia. Faces in the crowds twisted into grotesque masks, mirroring the malevolent force's influence. The challenges I faced resonated with the Weaver's dark artistry, each step a reflection of the nightmares Aria confronted in the heart of the cosmic labyrinth.

The nightmares had transcended Fantasia, infiltrating the waking world with an insidious presence.

Buildings contorted with the same surreal distortion, and shadows danced with purpose on the streets. The malevolent force's influence reached beyond the dreamlands, shaping the waking world into a reflection of cosmic horror.

–

As Daniel faced waking world challenges that mirrored the nightmares I endured, the strain on our symbiotic connection became palpable. The Weaver's influence permeated both realms, tightening the cosmic threads that bound our destinies. Daniel's challenges reflected the nightmares I navigated within Fantasia, creating a surreal echo of cosmic dissonance.

With each passing moment, the symbiotic connection strained under the weight of the Weaver's influence. The nightmares that unfolded in Fantasia now reverberated through the waking world, creating a symphony of discordant echoes. The cosmic threads that connected Daniel and me tightened, the strain on our connection becoming a palpable undercurrent in both realms.

The blurring of boundaries extended beyond the landscapes, reaching into the very essence of our beings. Daniel's waking world challenges were not mere reflections but intertwined manifestations of the nightmares that haunted Fantasia. The symbiotic connection, once a bridge between realms, now pulsed with the strain of cosmic forces at play.

—

As the nightmares in Fantasia echoed through the waking world, the strain on the symbiotic connection between Aria and me intensified. My challenges mirrored the cosmic discord within

Weaver's labyrinth, the threads of destiny tightening with Aria's struggles.

The blurring of boundaries extended beyond the surreal landscapes, weaving into the fabric of our shared existence. Each waking world challenge resonated with the nightmares that Aria confronted in Fantasia, creating a harmonious convergence of cosmic threads. The symbiotic connection, once a bridge between realms, now pulsed with the strain of interconnected destinies.

The Weaver's influence transcended the dreamlands, shaping the waking world into a reflection of cosmic horror. Every step I took mirrored Aria's journey through the distorted dreamscapes, the cosmic threads weaving our destinies together in a dance of nightmarish intricacy. The challenges intensified, reflecting the malevolent force's design within Fantasia and the strain on the symbiotic connection that bound Aria and me.

—

In the heart of the cosmic labyrinth, the nightmares that unfolded within Fantasia echoed through the waking world, creating a surreal echo of cosmic dissonance. Daniel's challenges mirrored the intricate scenarios that tested my resilience, blurring boundaries extending beyond the landscapes into the essence of our shared existence.

The strain on the symbiotic connection became a palpable undercurrent, resonating through both realms. The nightmares were not isolated to Fantasia; they manifested in the waking world, intertwining with the challenges Daniel confronted. The cosmic threads that bound us tightened in tandem, creating a symphony of discordant echoes reverberating through our interconnected destinies' surreal landscapes.

As Daniel navigated waking world challenges that mirrored my nightmares, Weaver's influence reached into the very core of our beings. The symbiotic connection, once a bridge between realms, now pulsed with the strain of cosmic forces at play. The surreal echo of cosmic dissonance became the soundtrack to our intertwined journey, a symphony of discord that unfolded within the cosmic tapestry of "The Everlasting Nightmare."

Chapter 13
Fraying Threads

In the heart of the cosmic labyrinth, the nightmares woven by the Weaver intensified, relentlessly testing my resilience to its limits. Once a realm of fantastical wonder, Fantasia now twisted into nightmarish landscapes, mirrored the malevolent force's attempt to unravel my mental and emotional resolve. Each nightmare felt like a cosmic tempest, threatening to tear apart the very fabric of my being.

As I traversed the distorted dreamscapes, the Weaver's malevolence manifested in every shadow and echo. The cosmic threads that bound my destiny were pulled taut, and the nightmares became intricate scenarios, each designed to dismantle the foundations of my strength. The weight of the Weaver's influence bore down on me like an unseen force, a relentless entity seeking to unravel the tapestry of my existence.

—

I witnessed Aria's valiant struggles against the Weaver's nightmares through the symbiotic connection. The surreal landscapes unfolded before me, reflecting the cosmic discord gripping Fantasia. Aria's resilience, once a shining beacon, was being tested. I felt the strain on the symbiotic threads that bound our destinies with each nightmare.

The shadows of doubt and fear that Aria confronted echoed through the connection, their insidious influence reaching the core of our shared existence. The Weaver's malevolence manifested not only in the dreamlands but also in the psychological toll it exacted on Aria. Each step she took, battling against the cosmic nightmares, resonated through the symbiotic connection, creating a symphony of discordant echoes reverberating through the cosmic tapestry.

—

As the nightmares unfolded, I confronted shadows of doubt and fear, manifestations of the Weaver's insidious influence. The internal struggle became palpable, a battle against the psychological toll exacted by the cosmic nightmares. The surreal landscapes twisted and contorted with each step, mirroring my mind's intricate dance of despair.

The cosmic threads that bound my destiny tightened, and the fraying edges threatened to unravel the very fabric of my being. The relentless onslaught of Weaver's nightmares sought to dismantle the foundations of my strength, pushing me to confront the shadows of doubt and fear that lurked within. Each step in Fantasia mirrored the internal struggle. This surreal ballet unfolded within the cosmic tapestry of "The Everlasting Nightmare."

—

I witnessed Aria's descent into the heart of the Weaver's nightmares through the symbiotic connection. The cosmic threads that bound our destinies vibrated with the strain of her internal struggle. Shadows of doubt and fear echoed through the connection, their insidious influence reaching the core of our shared existence.

Aria's resilience, once a beacon of strength, faced the relentless onslaught of the Weaver's malevolence. The fraying threads threatened to unravel the foundations of her mental and emotional resolve. With each nightmare, I felt the weight of the cosmic discord bearing down on her, pushing her closer to the brink of despair. The symbiotic connection became a conduit for the symphony of discordant echoes, each note a testament to Aria's internal struggle within the cosmic nightmare. The boundary between our realities blurred further as the cosmic forces tightened their grip, creating a nightmarish symphony that echoed through Fantasia and the waking world.

—

As I ventured deeper into Fantasia, the fragmented realities reached a breaking point, and the dreamlands seemed to unravel before my eyes. The cosmic disturbance tore at the very fabric of this once-vibrant realm, rendering landscapes into shards of fractured dreams. Every step became a precarious journey through the unraveling cosmic tapestry, the ground beneath me unstable and shifting like sand in the wind.

The surreal challenges intensified as the boundaries between dreams and nightmares blurred. The Weaver's malevolence echoed through the dissonant landscapes, creating a chaotic symphony that reverberated through the shattered realms of Fantasia. Each stride brought me closer to the heart of the cosmic tempest, where reality and unreality danced in a tumultuous ballet.

—

Through the symbiotic connection, I witnessed Fantasia's descent into chaos. Shattered landscapes unfolded before me, each fragment reflecting the cosmic dissonance that now gripped the dreamlands. Aria's journey through the unraveling tapestry mirrored the strain on our shared destinies, and the Weaver's malevolence echoed through the disintegrated dreamscapes.

As the boundaries between dreams and nightmares blurred, the dissonance intensified, creating a symphony of chaos that resonated through the connection. Fantasia, once a realm of wonder, now stood on the precipice of desolation. Aria's Every Step became a testament to the fragile nature of the cosmic tapestry, and the symbiotic threads that bound our destinies vibrated with the strain of the unraveling dreamscape.

—

In the heart of Fantasia's descent into chaos, I navigated through landscapes on the verge of collapse. The shattered dreamscape unfolded like a jigsaw puzzle of cosmic dissonance, each piece a reflection of the Weaver's malevolence. The ground beneath me felt treacherous, the essence of the dreamlands tearing at the seams.

The dissonance intensified as I faced surreal challenges; the boundaries between dreams and nightmares blurred into a chaotic symphony of cosmic discord. Every step resonated with the unraveling of the once-vibrant realm, and the echoes of desolation reverberated through the fraying cosmic tapestry. As I approached the heart of the cosmic tempest, the fragile nature of Fantasia became increasingly evident, and the symbiotic connection with Daniel tightened, a shared experience of navigating through the unraveling dreamscape.

–

I felt the strain of Fantasia's descent into chaos through the symbiotic connection. Shattered landscapes unfolded before me, each fragment reflecting Weaver's malevolence and the intensifying cosmic dissonance. Aria's journey through the unraveling dreamlands mirrored the strain on our shared destinies, and the boundaries between dreams and nightmares blurred into a chaotic symphony.

Aria's every step resonated through the connection as the cosmic tapestry unraveled, creating a shared descent into the heart of chaos. The once-vibrant Fantasia now stood on the precipice of desolation, and the symbiotic threads that bound our destinies vibrated with the strain of the unfolding cosmic tempest. The echoes of desolation reverberated through both realms, creating a surreal ballet of shared experiences within the unraveling dreamscape.

—

As I continued my journey through the shattered landscapes of Fantasia, the cosmic dissonance escalated, reaching a crescendo that reverberated through the dreamlands. Each step felt like a dance with chaos, and the echoes of desolation painted a vivid tapestry of cosmic unraveling. The heart of chaos loomed ahead, a surreal landscape where nightmares and dreams collided.

The Weaver's malevolence manifested in every shadow, and the shattered dreamscapes reflected the intricate threads woven by this sinister force. I faced surreal challenges, each more intricate and insidious than the last, testing my resolve and the fabric of the symbiotic connection that bound Daniel and me.

—

In the waking world, surreal intrusions disrupted the familiar rhythm of my reality. Moments of disorientation swept over me like waves, and the fractured landscapes of Fantasia bled into my surroundings. The cosmic threads wove through both realms, disorienting me as the waking world mirrored the chaotic dance of nightmares.

Echoes of Fantasia infiltrated my waking experiences, creating a surreal juxtaposition of realities. The strain on my perception intensified, and the symbiotic connection deepened, causing blurred lines between reality and cosmic disorientation. The waking world became a canvas where the echoes of Fantasia painted a surreal portrait of intertwined destinies.

—

As I approached the heart of chaos, the surreal challenges became more intricate and insidious. The shattered dreamscapes unfolded with nightmarish precision, reflecting the Weaver's malevolence. Every step tested my resolve, and the cosmic dissonance intensified, creating a symphony of chaos that echoed through the fraying cosmic tapestry.

The heart of chaos revealed itself as a surreal landscape where nightmares and dreams collided. Shadows of doubt and fear manifested, each confrontation pushing me closer to the brink. The relentless onslaught of Weaver's malevolence tested my mental and emotional resolve and the essence of the symbiotic connection that bound Daniel and me.

—

In the waking world, echoes of Fantasia infiltrated my reality. Surreal intrusions disrupted the familiar rhythm of my waking experiences, and moments of disorientation became a testament to the cosmic threads that linked both realms. The symbiotic connection deepened, causing blurred lines between reality and the surreal echoes of Fantasia.

As Fantasia's landscapes bled into the waking world, the strain on my perception intensified. The Weaver's influence reached beyond the dreamlands, creating a surreal juxtaposition in my waking reality. The waking world became a canvas where nightmares and dreams intertwined, and the cosmic disorientation echoed throughout my existence.

Chapter 14
Convergence of Nightmares

Determined to unravel the enigma of the Weaver of Nightmares, I pressed forward through the fractured dreamscapes, guided by an insatiable thirst for understanding. Shadows of despair clung to every step, but I forged ahead, seeking the heart of chaos where the Weaver's origins lay hidden.

The distorted landscapes mirrored the torment within me as I journeyed through the surreal and fractured dreamscape. Each step felt like a dance with the shadows, revealing glimpses of the Weaver's malevolent past. The very essence of Fantasia seemed to pulse with the echoes of the Weaver's sinister deeds.

Visions of ancient realms consumed by the Weaver's influence flashed before my eyes. Eldritch entities bowed to its cosmic malevolence, and the very fabric of Fantasia trembled under the weight of its dark artistry. As I delved into the history of the malevolent force, I discovered the Weaver's insidious roots, intertwined with forgotten nightmares that spanned epochs.

The revelation of the Weaver's enigmatic history was a harrowing journey, a descent into the abyss where cosmic horrors and forgotten nightmares merged into a tapestry of madness. Each revelation exposed the Weaver's motivations, its roots entwined with the darkest corners of the Dreamlands.

—

In the waking world, as Aria navigated the mysteries of the Dreamlands, I, too, felt the weight of her discoveries echoing through the symbiotic connection. The cosmic design unfolded before me, and Weaver's role in shaping the disturbance in the Dreamlands became apparent.

Aria's revelations seeped into my waking experiences, each puzzle piece altering the fabric of our intertwined destinies. The cosmic threads tightened as Aria uncovered the intricate connection between the Weaver and the disturbance in the Dreamlands. The newfound knowledge reverberated through the symbiotic connection, shaping my understanding of the cosmic nightmares that haunted Fantasia.

As Aria delved into Weaver's cosmic design, the boundaries between our experiences blurred, and the malevolent force's impact on Fantasia became a shared truth. The unveiling of the Weaver's role in the cosmic tapestry signaled a turning point in our journey, where the convergence of nightmares reached a crescendo.

The symbiotic connection intensified, and I immersed myself in the nightmares Aria confronted. The waking world became a distorted reflection of Fantasia's chaos, mirroring the malevolence that the Weaver had wrought upon the Dreamlands. Every waking moment became a surreal dance with shadows, a testament to the cosmic dissonance echoing through our shared destinies.

The revelation of the Weaver's cosmic design unveiled a path fraught with challenges, and the malevolent force's presence loomed over us like a dark omen. Aria's pursuit of truth brought us closer to the heart of cosmic nightmares and the blurred boundaries between dreams and reality. The symphony of our shared destinies played on, echoing through the ever-tightening threads of the Everlasting Nightmare.

―

The revelation of the Weaver's sinister past echoed through Fantasia, resonating with the very essence of the Dreamlands. As I pressed on, guided by the symbiotic connection that intertwined our fates, the nightmares in both realms began to converge with an eerie precision.

The nightmarish symmetry unfolded like a cosmic ballet, transcending the boundaries that separated Fantasia from the waking world. Every step I took in the Dreamlands echoed in the waking world, and Daniel, too, felt the inexorable pull of the nightmares weaving their intricate dance. The once-distinct realms blurred into a surreal amalgamation of cosmic horror.

The nightmares mirrored each other with uncanny precision, creating a synchronized descent into madness. Shadows danced in harmony, weaving a tapestry of despair transcending reality's very fabric. Aria and Daniel, both ensnared by the symphony of nightmares, faced challenges that mirrored the other's struggles, creating an intricate dance of cosmic dissonance.

As the convergence intensified, the boundaries between Fantasia and the waking world eroded, and the symbiotic connection reached a zenith. Each nightmarish encounter resonated through both realms, distorting the very essence of existence. The cosmic forces at play were orchestrating a symphony of descent, where the dance of nightmares transcended the limits of perception.

—

In the waking world, the nightmares that plagued Aria's journey seeped into my reality with an unsettling fluidity. The blurring of realms intensified as the convergence of nightmares eroded the barriers separating Fantasia from the waking world. Every dissonant note in Aria's struggles reverberated through my waking experiences, creating a surreal tapestry of cosmic horror.

The once-sturdy walls between the Dreamlands and reality crumbled, allowing the nightmares to intertwine in a macabre dance. I felt the pull of Fantasia, its distorted landscapes bleeding into the waking world. The very fabric of existence seemed to warp as if the cosmic forces were manipulating reality.

The tapestry of nightmares woven by the cosmic forces distorted the familiar landscapes of my waking experiences. Moments of disorientation became more frequent, and the surreal intrusions mirrored the nightmares that Aria confronted in Fantasia. The blurring of realms reached a point where the waking world became a distorted reflection of the cosmic dissonance echoing through the Everlasting Nightmare.

As Aria and I faced the convergence of nightmares, the symphony of descent played on, resonating through the unraveling threads of reality. The blurring of Fantasia and the waking world reached a crescendo, and the cosmic forces orchestrated a dance that transcended the boundaries of imagination, plunging us deeper into the unfathomable depths of the Everlasting Nightmare.

—

The nightmares entwined with the waking world, blurring the boundaries between Fantasia and reality. The parallel struggles Daniel and I faced grew more profound with each step, a testament to the symbiotic connection that bound us. Our challenges mirrored each other with an eerie precision, transcending mere influence to create a profound parallelism.

As I navigated the distorted landscapes of Fantasia, shadows of doubt and despair mirrored Daniel's waking world challenges. The cosmic resonance between our struggles intensified, echoing through both realms. The surreal ballet of nightmares became a shared experience. This haunting echo resonated through the very fabric of our intertwined destinies.

Every victory, defeat, and moment of despair and resilience reverberated through the symbiotic connection that transcended the boundaries of Fantasia and the waking world. The shared challenges forged a bond beyond understanding, pushing us to confront the cosmic forces orchestrating our destinies.

—

The nightmares, once confined to Fantasia, now bled into my waking world, creating a surreal fusion of dreams and reality. Aria and I faced shared challenges that echoed through both realms, intensifying the cosmic resonance that bound our fates together. The symbiotic connection reached its zenith, and the weight of our intertwined destinies pressed upon us with relentless force.

In the waking world, echoes of Aria's struggles manifested as surreal intrusions, blurring the line between reality and cosmic dissonance. The nightmares that unfolded in Fantasia mirrored my challenges, creating a profound parallelism that transcended the limits of imagination.

As the cosmic forces intensified, the dance of nightmares reached a crescendo, pushing us to the brink of our abilities. The symbiotic connection became a conduit for the total weight of our intertwined fates, and the boundaries between Aria and me blurred into a seamless tapestry of shared destinies.

The Everlasting Nightmare, with its echoes of destiny, unfolded with relentless momentum, propelling Aria and me toward an unknown conclusion. Now at their peak, the cosmic forces orchestrated a symphony of intertwining destinies, leaving us to navigate the intricate dance of nightmares that transcended the boundaries of Fantasia and the waking world.

Chapter 15

Whispers Across Realms

—

In the ever-shifting landscapes of Fantasia, the subtle shift in the cosmic currents became more pronounced. The first echoes of forgotten dreams, like delicate tendrils of ethereal mist, began to weave through the fabric of the dreamlands. As I journeyed through the surreal terrains, a sense of nostalgia and intrigue enveloped me, akin to the warmth of a long-lost memory returning.

The whispers from realms long past brushed against the edges of my consciousness, leaving an indelible imprint on the very essence of Fantasia.

Cryptic fragments of bygone dreams echoed through the cosmic tapestry, their enigmatic significance eluding easy interpretation. It was as if the very essence of this fantastical realm held memories that transcended time, waiting to be uncovered and understood.

In my quest to unravel the secrets of the Weaver of Nightmares, these echoes played a crucial role. They felt like keys, unlocking doors to forgotten corridors of cosmic history. Each step I took, guided by the mysterious resonance of these ancient dreams, led me closer to understanding the true nature of the cosmic disturbance that threatened Fantasia.

–

In the waking world, the sensation of blurred boundaries persisted, intensifying the revelation of intricate threads from the past. The cryptic fragments gained clarity, resonating with an otherworldly familiarity that tugged at the edges of my consciousness. Forgotten dreams whispered through the corridors of my mind, weaving an intricate tapestry of enigmatic nostalgia that seemed to transcend the limitations of ordinary time.

As I delved deeper into the echoes, the waking world transformed into a canvas painted with the hues of cosmic history. The resonance of these forgotten dreams shaped reality with a subtle but undeniable influence. It was as if the boundaries of time themselves were becoming malleable, allowing me glimpses into a cosmic history that held profound connections to the struggles of Fantasia.

The intertwining of Aria's and my experiences with these echoes marked a turning point in our cosmic journey. The Everlasting Nightmare held the echoes of our shared struggles and the resonance of dreams that had long faded into the tapestry of cosmic memory. The intricate threads of the past, now unraveled, promised revelations that would redefine the very nature of our intertwined destinies.

—

In the ever-shifting landscapes of Fantasia, the subtle shift in the cosmic currents became more pronounced. The first echoes of forgotten dreams, like delicate tendrils of ethereal mist, began to weave through the fabric of the dreamlands. As I journeyed through the surreal terrains, a sense of nostalgia and intrigue enveloped me, akin to the warmth of a long-lost memory returning.

The whispers from realms long past brushed against the edges of my consciousness, leaving an indelible imprint on the very essence of Fantasia. Cryptic fragments of bygone dreams echoed through the cosmic tapestry, their enigmatic significance eluding straightforward interpretation. It was as if the very essence of this fantastical realm held memories that transcended time, waiting to be uncovered and understood.

In my quest to unravel the secrets of the Weaver of Nightmares, these echoes played a crucial role. They felt like keys, unlocking doors to forgotten corridors of cosmic history. Each step I took, guided by the mysterious resonance of these ancient dreams, led me closer to understanding the true nature of the cosmic disturbance that threatened Fantasia.

—

In the waking world, the sensation of blurred boundaries persisted, intensifying the revelation of intricate threads from the past. The cryptic fragments gained clarity, resonating with an otherworldly familiarity that tugged at the edges of my consciousness. Forgotten dreams whispered through the corridors of my mind, weaving an intricate tapestry of enigmatic nostalgia that seemed to transcend the limitations of ordinary time.

As I delved deeper into the echoes, the waking world transformed into a canvas painted with the hues of cosmic history. The resonance of these forgotten dreams shaped reality with a subtle but undeniable influence. It was as if the boundaries of time themselves were becoming malleable, allowing me glimpses into a cosmic history that held profound connections to the struggles of Fantasia.

The intertwining of Aria's and my experiences with these echoes marked a turning point in our cosmic journey. The Everlasting Nightmare held the echoes of our shared struggles and the resonance of dreams that had long faded into the tapestry of cosmic memory.

The intricate threads of the past, now unraveled, promised revelations that would redefine the very nature of our intertwined destinies.

—

Cryptic messages embedded within the echoes served as a bridge between Fantasia and the waking world. The dream language, an intricate tapestry of symbols and metaphors, began to reveal itself to me. It was as if each symbolic thread held the key to unlocking the hidden meanings behind the fragmented memories that echoed through the cosmic currents.

With each deciphered message, the veil between realms thinned. The symbolic language of dreams became a conduit, allowing me to communicate not only with the forgotten echoes of Fantasia but also with Daniel in the waking world. The cryptic messages, once enigmatic whispers, transformed into a shared language that bound our fates together across the cosmic expanse.

–

Fragmented memories acted as a fractured mirror, reflecting glimpses of a forgotten reality. The waking world, once familiar and linear, now mirrored the shattered landscapes of Fantasia. As I unraveled the cryptic puzzle within the whispers, the fragments of memory transformed into a kaleidoscope of images, each piece contributing to the mosaic of our intertwined destinies.

Navigating the blurred lines between past and present became a surreal dance. The fractured mirror held reflections of ancient dreams and cosmic disturbances, creating a mosaic of interconnected moments. In these fragmented memories, the hidden truths of our cosmic journey lay, waiting to be uncovered and pieced together like a cosmic jigsaw puzzle.

Like a cosmic lullaby, the whispers and memories guided Aria and me through the intricacies of a reality woven from dreams and nightmares. The cryptic messages and fractured memories served as bridges, connecting our experiences across the vast tapestry of the Everlasting Nightmare.

—

As the echoes of forgotten dreams resonated through Fantasia, the eldritch entities, once silent observers, emerged as guardians of realms obscured by the mists of time. Their forms, nebulous and ever-shifting, radiated an aura of ancient wisdom. It was as if they existed beyond the boundaries of ordinary perception, their enigmatic presence transcending the very fabric of Fantasia.

"Seek the echoes," one entity intoned, echoing through the cosmic currents. "Follow the threads woven by forgotten dreams. Guardians, we are, of realms lost to the passage of eons. The convergence awaits."

Their cryptic guidance became a compass directing me through the kaleidoscopic landscapes. Each step was a journey through realms forgotten, guided by the elusive wisdom of these ancient entities. Their formless shapes pulsed with the energy of cosmic guardianship, urging me onward toward a convergence point where the echoes of ancient dreams intertwined.

–

In the waking world, the echoes resonated with equal potency, threading through the tapestry of reality like a cosmic heartbeat. The eldritch entities' presence transcending mortal understanding's limitations beckoned with cryptic urgency.

"Pursue the echoes," their voices echoed in harmonious unison. "In pursuit lies revelation, and in revelation, the dance of destinies."

Compelled by the enigmatic guidance, I felt an irresistible urge to follow the trails of forgotten dreams. The waking world became a realm of echoes and whispers, each step resonating with the cosmic forces that bound Aria and me together. The urgency of the pursuit heightened, and the threads of destiny tightened around us like the strings of a cosmic instrument.

The echoes, like a siren's call, propelled us forward. Aria and I, bound by the symbiotic connection, navigated through the intricacies of our respective realms, drawn inexorably toward the convergence point where the cryptic wisdom of the eldritch entities promised to unveil the secrets shrouded in the echoes of forgotten dreams.

—

The journey through Fantasia led me to a realm where the echoes converged, creating a cosmic symphony that resonated with the pulse of ancient dreams. The eldritch entities, now luminous beacons of enigmatic guidance, surrounded me in a kaleidoscope of cosmic energies.

"Behold the convergence," their voices echoed. "In the symphony of nightmares, truths shall be revealed."

As I stood at the epicenter of this cosmic convergence, the nightmares transformed into an intricate dance of shadows and light. The threads of destiny intertwined with the echoes, and the revelations echoed through the very fabric of Fantasia. The eldritch entities, guardians of forgotten realms, watched with an otherworldly intensity as the cosmic tapestry of our destinies unfolded.

—

In the waking world, the echoes led me to a place where reality and dreams melded into a surreal tapestry. The eldritch entities, their forms flickering like distant stars, stood as sentinels in this cosmic convergence.

"Threads unravel," they intoned, their voices weaving through the echoes. "In the unraveling, the truth shall be laid bare."

As Aria and I approached the convergence point, the boundaries between Fantasia and the waking world blurred even further. The cosmic forces intensified, and the threads of destiny tightened to their limits. The symphony of nightmares reached a crescendo, and at that moment, the enigmatic guidance of the eldritch entities became clear—the unveiling of truths awaited us at the crossroads of converging nightmares.

The dance of destinies, set in motion by the cosmic forces and guided by the eldritch entities, entered a phase where the echoes of forgotten dreams and the revelations of ancient nightmares converged in a cosmic ballet that transcended the boundaries of Fantasia and the waking world.

Chapter 16
Dreams in Tandem

The echoes, once subtle whispers, now pulsed with an undeniable urgency. Each encounter intensified, the cosmic beacons guiding me through the labyrinth of Fantasia's forgotten histories. The eldritch entities' cryptic guidance had led me to a realm where the echoes resonated with the power of ancient revelations.

"Seek the heart of echoes," the ethereal voices whispered. "In their resonance lies the key to unraveling the tapestry of cosmic nightmares."

As I followed the cosmic beacons, the dreamscape unfolded with kaleidoscopic brilliance. Fantasia, bathed in the celestial glow of echoes, revealed vistas of forgotten civilizations and landscapes lost to the sands of time. Each step was a journey through the annals of history, guided by the celestial rhythm that pulsed through the very fabric of Fantasia.

–

In the waking world, the echoes manifested as subtle intrusions that transcended the boundaries of reality. As I traversed the familiar streets, the sensory overload became palpable. The echoes amplified, creating a dreamscape that coexisted with the waking world.

The symphony of forgotten dreams played before me, shaping the environment with ethereal landscapes and resonant memories. Sensory boundaries blurred as the echoes immersed me in a surreal dreamscape that mirrored Aria's experiences in Fantasia. The streets I walked transformed into ancient thoroughfares, and the buildings echoed the whispers of civilizations long past.

Navigating this dreamscape became a sensory dance, an intricate ballet guided by cosmic forces. Aria and I, connected by the symbiotic thread, now traversed parallel realms where the echoes of forgotten dreams painted the canvas of our intertwined destinies.

—

The echoes led me to a celestial nexus, where the resonance of forgotten dreams reached its zenith. The cosmic beacons converged, creating a symphony that transcended the boundaries of Fantasia. As I stood in the epicenter of this ethereal convergence, the celestial rhythm pulsed through me, resonating with the very core of my being.

"Feel the heartbeat of Fantasia," the eldritch entities whispered. "In the rhythm of echoes, the past and present dance as one."

The dreamscape transformed into a celestial ballet, and I danced through the echoes, witnessing the rise and fall of civilizations, the echoes of triumphs and tragedies blending into a cosmic harmony. The celestial rhythm guided me toward revelations at the heart of Fantasia's forgotten histories.

–

In the waking world, the sensory overload peaked as the echoes painted the urban landscape with glimpses of ancient memories. The familiar surroundings melded with the dreamscape, and I navigated the juxtaposition of modernity and antiquity.

The echoes whispered tales of forgotten eras, shaping the waking world into a dreamscape of its own. Streets became thoroughfares of antiquity, and the cityscape echoed with the voices of long-lost civilizations. The sensory dance intensified as I moved through this surreal dreamscape, guided by the cosmic forces orchestrating Fantasia's convergence and the waking world.

Aria and I danced through parallel realms, united by the celestial rhythm that resonated through the echoes of forgotten dreams. The cosmic forces, once enigmatic and distant, now guided us toward the heart of revelations that awaited us in the intertwining tapestry of cosmic nightmares.

—

The celestial rhythm guided me through the convergence of echoes. The narrative threads interweaved as I delved deeper into Fantasia's forgotten history. The cosmic beacons acted as storytellers, painting vivid images in the tapestry of my mind. Each echo added a layer to the cosmic saga, and the fragmented memories formed a cohesive narrative that spanned epochs.

The whispers of the eldritch entities guided my understanding, revealing tales of ancient civilizations and cosmic disturbances that echoed through the ages. As the threads of the narrative intertwined, I saw the rise and fall of realms, the cosmic forces at play, and the profound impact of the Weaver of Nightmares on Fantasia's destiny.

–

In the waking world, the echoes manifested as whispers that unraveled the fabric of forgotten realities. The cityscape transformed into a gallery of vivid images, each echo painting a tableau of civilizations lost in the sands of time. The juxtaposition of modernity and antiquity blurred, and I witnessed the grandeur and tragedy of Fantasia's past.

The echoes unveiled forgotten realities, portraying the lives of those who once walked the same streets I now tread. I glimpsed ancient rituals, heard the echoes of laughter and sorrow, and witnessed the ebb and flow of Fantasia's cosmic pulse. The revelations within the echoes bridged the gap between epochs, connecting the present to the ancient tapestry of the Dreamlands.

—

As the narrative threads interwove, I stood at the heart of Fantasia, where the echoes converged into a celestial symphony. The eldritch entities' whispers reached a crescendo, and the cosmic beacons pulsed with the heartbeat of Fantasia.

"In the echoes, find the essence of Fantasia's resilience," the voices urged. "The threads of cosmic nightmares are woven into the very fabric of this realm."

The revelations unfolded like chapters in an ancient tome. Fantasia, a realm shaped by cosmic forces, witnessed cataclysms and rebirths. The heartbeat of the Dreamlands echoed through the narrative threads, connecting the destinies of its inhabitants to a cosmic design that transcended time.

—

In the waking world, the echoes guided me through the city's labyrinthine streets, revealing the essence of Fantasia's cosmic disturbance. The vivid images painted by the echoes depicted realms in upheaval, celestial forces colliding, and the unmistakable influence of the Weaver of Nightmares.

The revelations echoed Aria's experiences in Fantasia, creating a harmonious synergy between the cosmic disturbances in both realms. As the narrative threads intertwined, I felt the weight of the cosmic forces shaping the destiny of Fantasia and its inhabitants.

Aria and I uncovered the essence of Fantasia's resilience and vulnerability, woven into the cosmic tapestry through the echoes of forgotten dreams. The narrative threads painted a tableau of cosmic significance, urging us to delve deeper into the heart of revelations that awaited us in the unraveling cosmic saga.

—

As the echoes intensified, the voices of Eldritch allies and adversaries resonated within the cosmic narrative. Their enigmatic guidance transformed the echoes into a living chronicle, each voice contributing to the unfolding tale of Fantasia's forgotten history. Once distant and cryptic, the eldritch entities became storytellers shaping the cosmic saga.

"In the echoes, the voices of allies and adversaries converge. Listen, for their tales intertwine with the destiny of Fantasia," the eldritch entities whispered, their voices echoing through the cosmic tapestry.

The Eldritch allies, guardians of forgotten realms, spoke of their roles in preserving the balance within Fantasia. Adversaries from the cosmic abyss revealed their malevolent influence, entwined with the Weaver of Nightmares. The echoes painted a portrait of alliances forged in the crucible of cosmic turmoil and enmities that echoed through the ages.

—

In the waking world, the echoes acted as vessels for cosmic revelations. Eldritch voices, both allies and adversaries, unraveled mysteries that transcended mortal understanding. Each whisper carried the weight of eons, revealing the intricate web of destinies that wove Fantasia's tapestry.

Aria and I became conduits for the eldritch voices as I navigated the waking world, our destinies converging with the cosmic forces shaping the narrative. The echoes unveiled the cosmic dance of alliances and conflicts, and I sensed the profound impact of these revelations on the unfolding tale.

The eldritch entities guided us, urging us to embrace our roles in the cosmic symphony. Fantasia's forgotten history echoed through the ages. With each revelation, the protagonists stepped closer to understanding their place in the grand narrative of the Dreamlands.

—

"Guardians and adversaries, allies and foes, their voices weave the tale of Fantasia's resilience," the eldritch entities spoke in unison, their voices merging into a harmonious melody. "Embrace the echoes, for within them lies the wisdom of those who shaped the destiny of this realm."

The revelations unfolded like a celestial scroll, the wisdom of the Eldritch allies providing insights into the delicate balance that maintained Fantasia's existence. Adversaries, though malevolent, played integral roles in the cosmic narrative, and their motives echoed through the ages.

—

The eldritch revelations echoed within me as I navigated the waking world. Eldritch allies and adversaries, their voices entwined in the cosmic narrative, revealed the intricacies of Fantasia's tapestry. The cosmic revelations acted as threads, weaving together destinies transcending time and space.

As Aria and I embraced the echoes, the eldritch entities' guidance became clearer. Fantasia's tale was a living chronicle, and we, as conduits for the eldritch voices, held the key to unraveling the threads that bound the cosmic forces to our destinies.

The unfolding tale echoed through both realms, shaping the understanding of their roles in the cosmic symphony. The voices within the echoes guided Aria and Daniel toward a destiny intertwined with the essence of Fantasia's existence.

Chapter 17
Shattered Realities

As the echoes gained prominence, the boundaries between the waking world and Fantasia blurred into a celestial fusion of realities. Aria felt the ethereal currents pulling her between realms, each step resonating with the power of the echoes. The once-clear distinction between waking and dreaming became an abstract concept, overshadowed by the cosmic forces at play.

"Fantasia and the waking world, entwined in a dance of echoes. Our steps echo through both realms, shaping the very fabric of existence," the eldritch entities whispered, their voices guiding Aria through the cosmic convergence.

Navigating this confluence of realms felt both empowering and disorienting. Aria embraced the fluidity, allowing the echoes to guide her through landscapes that seamlessly shifted between the waking and dreamlike.

–

In the waking world, the echoes' prominence thinned the ethereal veil between dimensions. Daniel glimpsed into realms that had been concealed, his perception transcending the boundaries of mortal understanding. The echoes acted as a key, unlocking the hidden vistas of Fantasia and the waking world.

"The echoes weave a tapestry that transcends mortal perception. Embrace the blurred lines, for within them lies the truth of Fantasia's existence," the eldritch voices echoed in Daniel's mind.

The surreal convergence of waking and dreaming became more pronounced. Daniel's reality intertwined with echoes of Fantasia, creating a landscape where the familiar and the otherworldly coexisted. As the echoes guided him, Daniel felt the profound impact of the cosmic forces shaping the fabric of his waking experiences.

—

"The celestial fusion is a ballet of echoes, where the boundaries of reality blur into a cosmic dance," the eldritch entities spoke, their voices harmonizing with the echoes. Aria felt herself becoming a dancer in this cosmic ballet, her every movement resonating with the echo's power.

The landscapes shifted seamlessly between realms, each step a harmonious interplay between waking and dream. Aria embraced the fluidity, the echoes guiding her through surreal vistas that defied mortal comprehension.

—

The ethereal veil lifted further, revealing glimpses beyond the ordinary. Daniel's waking world experiences became a canvas painted with echoes, where the boundaries between realms were no longer rigid. The eldritch voices whispered ancient truths, unraveling the secrets concealed within the cosmic tapestry.

"I see the echoes shaping my reality, a convergence of Fantasia and waking. The blurred lines hold the key to understanding," Daniel mused as he navigated the shifting landscapes.

The prominence of echoes marked a transformative moment, where the protagonists were immersed in a cosmic ballet, each movement resonating with the power of the Eldritch entities and the forgotten histories of Fantasia.

—

Navigating the cosmic ballet, Aria and Daniel found themselves immersed in fragmented realities that mirrored the forgotten dreams within Fantasia. The ever-shifting dreamscapes painted vivid portraits of civilizations and landscapes lost to time.

"Each step echoes through the ruins of forgotten dreams, revealing tales etched into the fabric of Fantasia," the eldritch voices whispered, guiding Aria through landscapes that fluctuated between grandeur and desolation.

The dreamscapes were in constant flux, mirroring the rise and fall of ancient civilizations. Aria marveled at the echoes' ability to bring forth the essence of Fantasia's past as if the dreams that shaped the realm were reawakening.

—

Echoes guided Aria and Daniel through the whispers of the past, unraveling tales that echoed with the resonance of forgotten dreams. They deciphered the symbolic language of the echoes, piecing together the shattered realities of Fantasia's history.

"The echoes speak a language woven with cosmic threads, telling stories of triumph, tragedy, and the eternal dance between creation and destruction," Daniel mused as he moved through dreamscapes that pulsed with the echoes' power.

They felt an intimate connection to the tales within the echoes as if they were witnessing and participating in Fantasia's cosmic narrative. Aria and Daniel embraced the unfolding revelations, embarking on a journey through the fragmented realities that profoundly explored the realm's hidden past.

—

As Aria traversed the dreamscapes in flux, she felt the cosmic threads unraveling before her. The echoes revealed the intricate tapestry of Fantasia's history, with each thread representing a moment lost to time.

"I see the rise and fall of civilizations, the cosmic symphony echoing through the ages. Fantasia's past is a canvas painted with dreams and nightmares," Aria spoke softly, her words carried by the ethereal winds of the dreamscapes.

The whispers of the past became vivid tales, allowing Aria to witness the triumphs and tragedies that shaped Fantasia. The echoes guided her through landscapes where the cosmic forces danced, leaving imprints of forgotten dreams in their wake.

—

Daniel, too, deciphered the symbolic language of the echoes as he moved through the dreamscapes. Whispers of the past echoed in his mind, revealing the cosmic significance of each fragmented memory.

"The echoes are a mosaic of meanings, a symbolic language transcending mortal comprehension. Fantasia's history unfolds before us in a dance of forgotten dreams," Daniel remarked, his eyes reflecting the profound revelations.

Aria and Daniel navigated the fragmented realities together, unraveling the tales etched within the echoes and gaining insight into the cosmic design that shaped Fantasia's existence.

—

As Aria and Daniel ventured deeper into the dreamscapes, the echoes resonated with a cosmic power that surpassed mortal understanding. Eldritch forces, unseen puppeteers of cosmic threads, manipulated the echoes, weaving a tapestry that revealed more profound layers of the cosmic disturbance.

"I feel their influence, the eldritch forces orchestrating the dance of echoes. We are but pawns in their cosmic play, entangled in threads that stretch across realms," Aria murmured, her senses attuned to the unseen forces manipulating the very fabric of Fantasia.

The dreamscapes pulsed with eldritch energy, each echo a manifestation of the forces that transcended the boundaries between dreams and nightmares. Aria's connection to the cosmic threads intensified, making her acutely aware of the intricate puppetry that guided their journey.

—

The echoes unraveled the tapestry of the cosmic disturbance, exposing the intricacies of Fantasia's connection to the Dreamlands and the waking world. Eldritch revelations unfolded before Daniel's eyes, each echo peeling back layers of cosmic truth.

"These echoes are keys to understanding the cosmic design, unraveling the tapestry that binds Fantasia to realms beyond mortal perception," Daniel spoke, his voice resonating with a newfound awareness.

As the eldritch puppeteers manipulated the echoes, Daniel and Aria delved deeper into the mysteries of the Dreamlands. The hidden truths revealed by the echoes reshaped their understanding of the cosmic forces at play, marking a pivotal moment in their journey through the shattered realities.

—

Aria sensed the eldritch forces at play, their puppetry intertwining cosmic threads that connected Fantasia to realms beyond. The echoes became conduits of revelation, guiding her through the unraveling tapestry of the cosmic disturbance.

"We dance to the whims of forces that shape the very fabric of reality. The echoes are our guide, but the puppeteers remain veiled in mystery," Aria whispered, her steps echoing through landscapes where the eldritch forces wove threads of cosmic significance.

The revelations unfolded like chapters in an eldritch tome, each echo contributing to the ever-expanding narrative that revealed Fantasia's role in the grand tapestry of existence.

—

Daniel, too, felt the influence of the eldritch puppeteers as the echoes exposed hidden truths. The unraveling tapestry laid bare the intricate connections between Fantasia, the Dreamlands, and the waking world.

"Our journey is a quest for understanding, for unraveling the cosmic threads that bind us to destinies beyond our grasp. The echoes guide us, but what lies beyond their manipulation?" Daniel pondered, his gaze fixed on the cosmic tapestry before him.

As Aria and Daniel navigated the dreamscapes, the revelations of the eldritch puppetry intensified, marking a point of no return in their quest to decipher the enigmatic echoes and the deeper layers of the cosmic disturbance.

Chapter 18
Resonance of the Past

As we delved into the echoes, the dreams of Fantasia unfolded like a celestial panorama before us. Timeless visions swept us away, carrying us through pivotal moments that resonated with the very essence of this cosmic realm.

"I see civilizations rising and falling, each moment etched into the fabric of Fantasia. The echoes unveil the grand tapestry of the Dreamlands, and we are witnesses to its profound history," Aria spoke, her voice tinged with awe as the visions unfolded around us.

The echoes guided us through corridors of forgotten dreams, revealing the untold stories of this mystical realm. Aria's connection with the cosmic threads deepened, allowing her to perceive the resonance of the past in vivid detail.

—

The echoes painted a cosmic panorama, each moment in Fantasia's history contributing to the vast tapestry of the Dreamlands. Aria and I navigated through these echoes like celestial archaeologists, unraveling the mysteries embedded within the resonance of the past.

"These visions are like fragments of a cosmic puzzle, each piece revealing a chapter in the history of Fantasia. We are privileged witnesses to the ebb and flow of civilizations, caught in the currents of time," I remarked, my senses attuned to the echoes guiding our journey.

As the timeless visions unfolded, Aria and I stood at the intersection of past and present, absorbing the profound resonance that echoed through the corridors of Fantasia. The cosmic narrative expanded, and with each revelation, the true significance of our intertwined destinies became clearer.

–

The echoes continued to guide us through the corridors of Fantasia's history, weaving revelations that challenged the very foundations of our understanding. As the visions unfolded, hidden truths surfaced, shattering illusions and reshaping the narrative of our cosmic journey.

"I thought I knew Fantasia, but these echoes reveal a deeper reality that defies expectations. The hidden truths are like celestial keys, unlocking the mysteries that have long been concealed within the cosmic tapestry," Aria remarked, her eyes reflecting a blend of wonder and contemplation.

The revelations within the echoes unfolded like chapters of an ancient tome, each page turned, bringing us closer to a profound understanding of our roles in this cosmic drama.

—

A paradigm shift washed over us as the revelations within the echoes challenged our preconceptions. The fabric of our understanding unraveled, exposing the intricate threads that bound Fantasia, the Dreamlands, and the waking world.

"These revelations redefine our purpose within this cosmic drama. It's not just about confronting nightmares or unraveling mysteries; it's about understanding our place in a grander narrative shaped by the echoes of forgotten dreams," I observed, my mind grappling with the weight of destiny.

As Aria and I stood on the precipice of a new understanding, the echoes resonated with the essence of forgotten dreams, urging us to embrace the profound significance of our intertwined fates. The cosmic forces that had guided us thus far unveiled a greater purpose—a purpose intricately connected to the heartbeat of Fantasia's past.

—

The ethereal guidance of the eldritch entities propelled us forward, navigating celestial currents within the echoes. It was as if the very fabric of Fantasia responded to their presence, guiding us toward the heart of the cosmic unraveling.

"These celestial currents carry the weight of untold secrets. We're on the brink of something monumental, and these entities are our celestial guides through the echoes," Aria mused, her gaze fixed on the cosmic tapestry that shimmered with wonder and foreboding.

The journey through the currents felt like a dance, a delicate ballet with cosmic forces. As we ventured more deeply, the echoes whispered secrets that resonated with the cosmic rhythms, hinting at the origins of the disturbance that threatened to reshape our intertwined destinies.

—

The eldritch entities revealed themselves as guardians of cosmic secrets, their enigmatic presence resonating with the echoes of forgotten dreams. A fragile alliance formed as Aria and I recognized these beings' pivotal role in the cosmic narrative.

"Their knowledge is key to unraveling the mysteries that bind Fantasia and the waking world. We stand at the threshold of revelation, and these entities are our guides through the cosmic labyrinth," I remarked, sensing the weight of responsibility that came with the newfound alliance.

As we followed the celestial currents, the guardians of cosmic secrets led us closer to the epicenter of the disturbance—a place where the cosmic threads intertwined, weaving a tale that transcended mortal comprehension. The heart of the cosmic unraveling awaited, and with every step, our destinies became more entwined with the cosmic forces that shaped Fantasia's fate.

Part III
Symphony of Madness

Chapter 19
The Dreamlands' Labyrinth

The journey into the heart of the Dreamlands was fraught with cosmic shadows, each step resonating with the thin veil that separated reality from unreality. As I ventured more deeply, the weight of the cosmic forces enveloped me, a cloak of shadows that whispered ancient secrets.

"The Dreamlands, a tapestry woven with cosmic threads, holds the key to unraveling the Symphony of Madness. But traversing this labyrinth demands more than mere courage," I murmured, acknowledging the perilous nature of my quest.

The cosmic shadows played tricks on perception, distorting the boundaries between dream and nightmare. Each stride forward felt like a dance with the unknown, a delicate ballet across the shifting landscapes of unreality.

—

Surreal landscapes unfolded around Aria, shifting and morphing in response to the cosmic disturbance that echoed through the Dreamlands. It was as if the very fabric of this otherworldly realm responded to the unseen forces, guiding Aria through a labyrinth of ethereal vistas.

"Fantasia and the Dreamlands share a kinship, their destinies intertwined by cosmic design. Aria walks a path that mirrors our shared struggles, navigating the shifting landscapes that reflect the chaos within," I observed, sensing the profound connection between

Aria's journey and the unraveling Symphony of Madness.

Aria delved deeper into the Dreamlands' labyrinth; the cosmic shadows whispered cryptic truths, hinting at her role in the unfolding cosmic narrative. The heart of the Dreamlands awaited, veiled in mystery and cosmic resonance.

—

The cosmic shadows clung to me like an ethereal shroud in the heart of the Dreamlands. The enigmatic forms of eldritch entities emerged, their ever-changing shapes guiding me through surreal landscapes that defied mortal comprehension.

"These guardians of forgotten realms, their essence shifting like whispers on the wind, guide me through the tapestry of cosmic existence," I mused, feeling a strange kinship with the entities as they navigated the intricacies of the Dreamlands.

The otherworldly guides, their cosmic wisdom etched into the fabric of their ever-changing forms, spoke in riddles that echoed through the celestial corridors. I trusted their cryptic guidance, knowing that the answers to the Symphony of Madness lay hidden within the cosmic dance we embarked upon.

—

As Aria ventured deeper into the Dreamlands, the eldritch entities served as celestial waypoints, marking the nexus of cosmic energies pulsating with the sleeping god's disturbance. Each step resonated with the delicate balance of the Dreamlands, a cosmic pilgrimage guided by forces beyond mortal understanding.

"The Dreamlands, where realities converge and diverge, becomes a canvas for Aria's journey. These celestial waypoints, pulsing with the essence of cosmic disturbance, mark the intersections of fate and destiny," I observed, sensing the profound significance of Aria's path.

The Dreamlands unfolded like an intricate tapestry, and as Aria followed the enigmatic guides through celestial waypoints, the echoes of forgotten dreams resonated with a celestial rhythm. The Symphony of Madness played on, and the cosmic pilgrimage deepened, unraveling the secrets that bound Fantasia to the Dreamlands and the waking world.

–

The labyrinthine passages of the Dreamlands resonated with unearthly music. This dissonant harmony seemed to emanate from the very fabric of the cosmos. The haunting notes accompanied me like a persistent background, each chord echoing the disturbance in the sleeping god's dreamscape.

"The music, a cosmic symphony of discordant notes, guides me through the intricate dance of the Dreamlands. Each dissonant harmony is a thread woven into the tapestry of the ever-unraveling cosmic narrative," I reflected, my senses attuned to the unsettling melodies that echoed through the celestial corridors.

The labyrinth responded to the music, its shifting landscapes morphing with cosmic dissonance. Every step I took was a dance with haunting notes, a journey more profound into the heart of the Dreamlands, where the Symphony of Madness played on.

For me, the haunting melodies served as a sign of the sleeping god's disturbance. As Aria traversed the labyrinth, the intensity of the music correlated with the unraveling fabric of the Dreamlands. Each note echoed the cosmic peril that threatened to consume both realms, and I felt the weight of the disturbance pressing upon me.

"The music, a celestial lament, is a guide and a warning. Its intensity reflects the very pulse of the Dreamlands, resonating with the cosmic forces that shape the fate of Fantasia and the waking world," I noted, my senses heightened to the dissonant symphony that wove through the tapestry of realities.

As Aria navigated the labyrinth with the haunting melodies as her guide, I couldn't shake the feeling that the music held secrets, cryptic messages hidden within the harmonies that could unravel the mysteries of the Symphony of Madness.

Chapter 20
Melodies of Madness

The labyrinth's dissonant symphony reached a crescendo as I encountered Eldritch beings, embodiments of the disturbing music that echoed through the Dreamlands. Their forms seemed to shift and contort with each note, an unsettling dance of sonic despair.

"These entities, living echoes of the eldritch symphony, stand as guardians of the Dreamlands' dissonant melodies. Their presence amplifies the cosmic disturbance. I find myself entangled in a surreal dance with these manifestations of the sleeping god's nightmares," I observed, my senses overwhelmed by the pulsating rhythm surrounding me.

Interrupted with the unsettling harmony, the Eldritch beings revealed cryptic glimpses of the Dreamlands' cosmic tapestry. As I faced them, I understood that they were more than mere guardians; they were keys to unlocking the deeper layers of the Symphony of Madness.

–

Through the symbiotic connection, I felt Aria's encounter with the Eldritch beings, and the cosmic shadows pulsated in response to the disturbing music. It was as if the very fabric of Fantasia resonated with the rhythm of the Dreamlands' dissonance.

"Aria, entangled in a surreal dance with these Eldritch beings, unveils the embodiment of the sleeping god's nightmares. The cosmic shadows pulsate to the rhythm of the disturbing music, revealing the intricate connection between the Dreamlands and our waking world," I mused, my perception blurred by the ethereal dance played out in the intertwined realms.

The Eldritch beings, guardians and embodiments of sonic despair, held the key to unraveling the Symphony of Madness's mysteries. As Aria faced this otherworldly encounter, I braced myself for the revelations that awaited, knowing that our destinies were intricately bound to the cosmic forces at play.

—

The disturbing music within the Dreamlands intensified, reaching a crescendo that echoed through the labyrinth. The discordant notes reverberated, causing disorientation and hallucinations to weave through the very fabric of this surreal realm. As I pressed forward, each step became a struggle against the overwhelming cacophony that threatened to unravel my grasp on reality.

"The music reaches a crescendo, a symphony of cosmic discord that distorts the Dreamlands itself. Disorientation sets in, and hallucinations dance at the edge of my perception. Navigating through these shifting realities becomes a harrowing journey, where the boundaries between real and illusion blur into a nightmarish tapestry," I narrated, my senses ensnared by the surreal landscape that unfolded before me.

—

Through our shared connection, I felt Aria's struggle against the crescendo of cosmic discord. The hallucinatory landscapes that unfolded mirrored the upheaval within the Dreamlands, and the very fabric of Fantasia quivered in response.

"As Aria moves deeper into the Dreamlands, the dissonant music manifests hallucinatory landscapes. The boundaries between reality and illusion blur, reflecting the cosmic upheaval orchestrated by the sleeping god's disturbed dreams. Each step becomes a descent into madness, a journey through the surreal realms shaped by the discordant symphony," I reflected, my perception wavering as the cosmic forces manipulated the tapestry of both realms.

As Aria faced the harrowing effects of the intensified music, I braced myself for the unknown challenges that awaited, knowing that the echoes of forgotten dreams held the key to unraveling the Symphony of Madness.

—

As I navigated the disorienting landscapes within the Dreamlands, I couldn't shake the feeling that the echoes of the eldritch symphony were reaching beyond Fantasia. The unsettling notes seemed to transcend the boundaries, seeping into the waking world where Daniel grappled with his understanding of the cosmic upheaval.

"The echoes of the eldritch symphony reverberate through the Dreamlands and into the waking world. Daniel, in his reality, senses the growing cosmic upheaval as these haunting notes tether his consciousness to the unfolding events within Fantasia," I narrated, a sense of foreboding accompanying each step I took.

—

In the waking world, I felt an ominous resonance building within me, a subconscious awareness of the eldritch symphony influencing both realms. The echoes acted as a haunting prelude to the events unfolding in Fantasia, connecting my waking consciousness to Aria's perilous journey.

"As the eldritch symphony echoes through my waking reality, I become a vessel for the haunting notes. The ominous resonance deepens my connection to Aria's journey. I feel the cosmic forces converging in a symphony of madness that transcends both the Dreamlands and the waking world," I reflected, grappling with the profound weight of our intertwined destinies.

As Aria and I moved closer to the heart of the Dreamlands, the echoes intensified, creating a cosmic harmony that resonated through the fabric of existence. The Symphony of Madness played on, and the threads of our fates intertwined amidst the dissonant notes.

Chapter 21
The Unseen Conductor

The veil between realms pulsed with palpable tension as I ventured deeper into the heart of the Dreamlands. The ethereal landscapes shifted around me, revealing hidden passages that seemed to guide my steps toward an unseen force—an unseen conductor orchestrating the cosmic symphony.

"As I traverse the labyrinthine realms, the cosmic tension thickens. The unseen conductor's influence becomes more apparent, shaping the very fabric of the Dreamlands. Each step brings me closer to the source of the disturbance, the veil pulsating with the enigmatic power that orchestrates this cosmic unraveling," I narrated, my senses attuned to the surreal dance of cosmic forces.

In the waking world, the echoes of the sleeping god resonated through my reality, serving as ethereal breadcrumbs leading Aria to the epicenter of the cosmic unraveling. Each manifestation of the sleeping god's nightmares unveiled fragments of the eldritch symphony's purpose, heightening my awareness of the interconnected destinies at play.

"As the echoes guide Aria through the Dreamlands, I sense the presence of the sleeping god's nightmares in my waking reality. The ethereal breadcrumbs lead her closer to the source, and with each encounter, the purpose behind the eldritch symphony becomes clearer, intertwining our fates in ways I'm only beginning to understand," I reflected, feeling the weight of cosmic forces converging.

As Aria and I moved forward, the echoes of the sleeping god's nightmares intensified, forming a celestial chorus that resonated through the Dreamlands. The purpose of this cosmic unraveling became a haunting melody. The unseen conductor's influence loomed more prominent with every step, shrouded in cosmic mystery.

–

Once a dissonant backdrop, the eldritch music began to take on a purposeful quality, its harmonies weaving a malevolent tapestry that orchestrated nightmares and realities within Fantasia. As I delved deeper into the Dreamlands, I witnessed the symbiotic dance between the eldritch beings and the cosmic symphony. Each note resonated with a sinister intent, shaping the destiny of Fantasia with a purpose that transcended the mere whims of the sleeping god.

"The eldritch music, once a cacophony, now resonates with purpose. Its harmonies orchestrate the nightmares and realities within Fantasia, shaping the very fabric of the Dreamlands. The malevolent intent behind each note becomes clearer as I navigate through the surreal landscapes, feeling the cosmic forces at play," I recounted, my steps guided by the haunting melodies that echoed through the labyrinthine realms.

–

In the waking world, I felt the repercussions of the purposeful harmonies echoing through Fantasia. The once clear boundaries between dreams and nightmares blurred as the eldritch music conducted a nightmarish tapestry transcending the conventional understanding of reality. Each note was a brushstroke painting of a surreal landscape where the cosmic forces played out their symphony of madness.

"The eldritch music shapes a nightmarish tapestry within Fantasia. The boundaries between dreams and nightmares blur as the sinister conductor orchestrates the cosmic symphony. The surreal landscapes painted by the harmonies challenge the very essence of reality, mirroring the intricate dance within the Dreamlands," I mused, feeling the cosmic dissonance intensify in both realms.

As Aria and I traversed the ever-shifting Dreamlands, the purposeful harmonies guided us toward the unseen conductor who orchestrated the cosmic unraveling. With each step, the malevolent intent of the eldritch music etched its mark on Fantasia, the nightmarish tapestry weaving a narrative of cosmic upheaval and impending doom.

—

In the quiet solitude of my study, the pages of "The Everlasting Nightmare" whispered secrets that transcended the boundaries of mere fiction. The words held a power I hadn't fathomed before—a ritual within the narrative that could bridge the realms between Fantasia and the waking world. As I delved deeper into the text, a cosmic revelation unfolded.

"Within the pages of 'The Everlasting Nightmare,' I unveil a cosmic secret—a ritual that could be the key to connecting Fantasia and the waking world. The words on these pages hold a power that resonates with the eldritch symphony. I find myself drawn into a role beyond mere storytelling," I murmured, the weight of cosmic awareness settling on my shoulders.

—

As Daniel deciphered the enigmatic rituals within the book's pages, a revelation echoed through the Dreamlands. The ritual, intricately described within "The Everlasting Nightmare," became a potential bridge between realms—a metaphysical link capable of altering the very course of the cosmic disturbance that threatened Fantasia. I felt the cosmic threads tighten as Daniel grappled with the profound knowledge embedded in the narrative.

"The ritual, unveiled within the words of 'The Everlasting Nightmare,' holds the potential to bridge the realms between Fantasia and the waking world. The metaphysical connection it promises could reshape the cosmic forces at play. Daniel's awareness of this ritual, his understanding of its significance, reverberates through the cosmic symphony," I mused, sensing the delicate dance of destiny weaving its intricate patterns.

The weight of the revelation pressed upon me as I grappled with the knowledge of the ritual. Every word I read seemed to resonate with the eldritch symphony, and I couldn't shake the awareness that my actions in the waking world held consequences that echoed through Fantasia. The lines between author and character blurred, and I was at the cosmic significance crossroads.

"The ritual within 'The Everlasting Nightmare' is a double-edged sword. It has the power to bridge the realms, yet the consequences are shrouded in cosmic uncertainty. As the one who holds the key, I wrestle with the knowledge that my actions in the waking world could shape the fabric of Fantasia's destiny," I whispered, my gaze fixed on the pages that seemed to pulse with a cosmic heartbeat.

Chapter 22
The Bridge Between Realms

The echoes guided me through the labyrinthine Dreamlands, each step resonating with purposeful harmonies that heralded an imminent cosmic confrontation. As I traversed the shifting landscapes, the very essence of Fantasia seemed to pulse with anticipation. The dissonant notes of the eldritch symphony grew more pronounced, leading me toward the heart of the disturbance.

The veil of cosmic tension thickened as I confronted the sleeping god—a colossal entity embodying the eldritch symphony. Its form undulated with the dissonant melodies that shaped the destiny of Fantasia. I stood resolute, gazing into the cosmic abyss that mirrored the sleeping god's gaze.

"The echoes have guided me to the epicenter of the cosmic disturbance, where the sleeping god awaits. The embodiment of the eldritch symphony stands before me, a colossal force that threatens to unravel the fabric of Fantasia and the waking world. The cosmic confrontation is inevitable, and I am but a small yet determined figure in the grand tapestry of destiny," I whispered, my words woven into the harmonies that reverberated through the Dreamlands.

—

The eldritch music intensified, reaching a crescendo that echoed through the Dreamlands like a symphony of cosmic discord. The dissonant notes vibrated through the fabric of Fantasia, and I felt the weight of the realm's destiny converging upon me. As I stood at the precipice of the cosmic confrontation, the harmonies seemed to acknowledge my presence, weaving a narrative that intertwined with the eldritch crescendo.

"I am the focal point of this cosmic drama, standing at the nexus of realms, where the eldritch music orchestrates the fate of Fantasia. The crescendo envelopes me, resonating with every fiber of my being. In this pivotal moment, I am not merely an observer but an active participant in the unfolding symphony of madness," I declared, my voice merging with the haunting melodies surrounding me.

—

In the waking world, the echoes of the eldritch symphony reverberated through my consciousness. The dissonant notes served as an ominous prelude to the cosmic drama unfolding within Fantasia. The awareness of Aria's confrontation with the sleeping god echoed through the eldritch symphony, tethering my waking consciousness to the cosmic disturbance.

"The echoes of the eldritch symphony bind me to Aria's cosmic confrontation. The dissonant notes serve as ethereal threads connecting the waking world to the Dreamlands. As I grapple with the knowledge of the ritual, I sense the impending climax of the cosmic drama. My role in it becomes clearer," I murmured, my senses attuned to the harmonies that transcended the boundaries between realms.

—

As I confronted the sleeping god at the heart of the Dreamlands, a celestial harmony unfolded around me. Eldritch entities emerged from the cosmic shadows, their forms ever-changing as they joined the cosmic symphony. Their otherworldly voices harmonized with the dissonant notes, creating a celestial counterforce that resonated through Fantasia.

"The eldritch entities, once enigmatic guides, now participate in the cosmic symphony. Their celestial harmony intertwines with the dissonant notes, creating a mesmerizing dance of cosmic forces. Together, we stand as a united front against the disturbance that threatens to unravel the fabric of Fantasia," I mused, feeling the weight of the cosmic confrontation.

–

The eldritch entities engaged in a surreal dance, their movements synchronized with the cosmic symphony. As they wove a tapestry of reality and unreality, the essence of Fantasia became a canvas for their ritualistic performance. The dance of eldritch shadows unfolded like a cosmic ballet, each movement designed to pacify the sleeping god.

"The dance of eldritch shadows takes on a profound purpose. With each step, they weave a tapestry that transcends the boundaries between dreams and nightmares. It's a ritual to restore cosmic balance. This dance echoes through the corridors of the Dreamlands and resonates with the heart of the disturbance," I reflected, my gaze fixed upon the celestial ballet.

—

In the waking world, the echoes of the eldritch symphony painted a vivid dreamscape before me. I witnessed Aria's confrontation with the sleeping god and the ethereal dance of the eldritch entities. The celestial harmony reached across realms, and I sensed its profound impact on Fantasia and the waking world.

"The celestial ballet unfolds before me, a surreal spectacle that transcends the boundaries of the Dreamlands. The eldritch symphony, once a harbinger of cosmic disturbance, now becomes a source of restoration. As the dance of eldritch shadows captivates both realms, I understand the intricate connection between Aria's actions in the Dreamlands and the cosmic balance that envelopes us all," I whispered, my consciousness tethered to the unfolding cosmic drama.

—

As the celestial harmony resonated through the Dreamlands, I felt a shift in the cosmic currents. In the waking world, Daniel had become a metaphysical conduit guided by the ritual. The echoes whispered of his transformation, and I marveled at the profound connection we now shared.

"The ritual, a bridge between realms, has transformed Daniel into a metaphysical conduit. He stands at the intersection of waking and dreaming, a vessel channeling the eldritch symphony from one reality to another. In this cosmic dance, our fates intertwine, and the balance teeters on the edge of restoration," I contemplated, my eyes fixed on the surreal ballet unfolding around me.

–

As I confronted the sleeping god, I sensed Daniel channeling the eldritch symphony from the waking world to Fantasia. His actions echoed through the Dreamlands, the cosmic energies flowing through him like a river of ethereal power. The balance began to shift, and I understood the weight of Daniel's role in this cosmic drama.

"Daniel, the conduit between realms, channels the eldritch symphony with a purpose. His influence extends beyond the waking world, reaching into the very fabric of the Dreamlands. The cosmic energies surge through him, weaving a tapestry that intertwines with the dance of eldritch shadows. Together, we navigate the delicate threads that bind our destinies," I thought, witnessing the cosmic convergence.

–

In the waking world, I embraced the role thrust upon me by the ritual. Becoming a metaphysical conduit, I felt the cosmic energies flow through me, guided by the echoes of the eldritch symphony. Each action and thought resonated with cosmic significance as I channeled the otherworldly forces into Fantasia.

"As the conduit between realms, I become a bridge of cosmic significance. The eldritch symphony courses through me, and I sense its impact on Fantasia. My connection to Aria deepens, and I understand my pivotal role in restoring the balance disrupted by the sleeping god's awakening. The echoes guide my every step, and I walk the fine line between waking and dreaming, tethered to a destiny entwined with Aria's," I murmured, feeling the weight of the cosmic forces converging within me.

Chapter 23
Symphony Unleashed

As I stood before the sleeping god, the echoes guided me through the cosmic symphony reaching its zenith. The harmonious crescendo echoed through Fantasia and the waking world, intertwining the realms in a dance of cosmic convergence.

"The symphony reaches its zenith, a harmonic crescendo that transcends the boundaries between waking and dreaming. The sleeping god stirs, and the ethereal notes reshape the very essence of Fantasia and the waking world. The echoes lead me through the cosmic upheaval, a witness to the profound harmony that defies mortal comprehension," I thought, my senses attuned to the ethereal waves washing over me.

In the waking world, I felt the surreal waves of the cosmic symphony altering the fabric of reality itself. The echoes guided my actions, and I marveled at the ethereal dance playing out across Fantasia and the waking world.

"The cosmic symphony's ethereal waves wash over both realms, altering the very essence of reality. I sense Aria's presence in Fantasia, and our destinies entwine in the cosmic upheaval. The echoes guide me through the surreal landscape of the waking world, and I become a conduit for the harmonious convergence that reshapes our shared reality," I pondered, aware of the cosmic forces at play.

As the cosmic symphony unfolded, I sensed Daniel's presence like a distant echo. Our destinies entwined in the harmonious convergence, creating a connection that surpassed the boundaries of Fantasia and the waking world.

"Daniel, a fellow traveler through the cosmic upheaval, his actions resonating with the symphony's ethereal waves. Our destinies entwined, we navigate the surreal landscapes shaped by the harmonious convergence. The echoes guide us both, and together, we stand at the precipice of a reality reshaped by the cosmic forces at play," I reflected, feeling the profound connection between us.

—

In the waking world, I moved with purpose, aware that each action echoed in Fantasia. The cosmic symphony's harmonious convergence became a tapestry of intertwined destinies, and I embraced the role of a participant in this cosmic drama.

"As the symphony reaches its zenith, I am a witness to the cosmic convergence that reshapes reality. Aria and I, connected by the echoes, stand at the center of this ethereal dance. The harmonious waves of the cosmic symphony guide my steps, and I move with the awareness that our destinies are entwined in the fabric of Fantasia and the waking world," I mused, feeling the profound impact of the cosmic forces upon our intertwined destinies.

—

In the heart of Fantasia, the eldritch forces responded to the cosmic symphony with a chaotic dance. Their movements mirrored the dissonant notes, creating a nightmarish spectacle that defied the laws of reality.

"The eldritch entities respond to the music with a dance that mirrors the dissonant notes. Chaos unfolds around me as their movements become conduits for cosmic energies. The very fabric of Fantasia warps and twists in response to the chaotic dance, and I navigate through nightmarish distortions that threaten to consume the realms," I thought, my every step accompanied by the unsettling rhythm of the eldritch response.

—

In the waking world, I witnessed the devastation spreading across reality itself. The eldritch response to the symphony disrupted the delicate balance between waking and dreaming, and chaos manifested in nightmarish distortions.

"The devastation is palpable, a ripple effect spreading across both Fantasia and the waking world. Nightmarish landscapes morph into surreal nightmares, and the foundations of reality crumble under the chaotic influence of the cosmic disturbance. I grapple with the profound impact of the eldritch response, realizing that my actions in the waking world have consequences that reverberate through both realms," I contemplated, aware of the destructive power unleashed by the cosmic symphony.

—

As I navigated through Fantasia, the nightmarish distortions intensified. The once-familiar landscapes twisted into surreal nightmares, and the very foundations of this dream realm crumbled under the overwhelming influence of the eldritch response.

"Reality warps and bends, nightmarish distortions consuming Fantasia. The echoes guide me through this surreal nightmare, and I witness the devastating impact of the eldritch response. The once-stable foundations of this dream realm crumble, and I press forward, driven by the urgency to confront the source of the cosmic disturbance," I thought, determination fueling my journey through the chaos.

–

In the waking world, the consequences of the eldritch symphony became apparent. Nightmarish distortions manifested, challenging the very fabric of reality. I grappled with the realization that my actions, guided by the ritual, played a part in unleashing this chaos.

"As the symphony's consequences unfold, I confront the devastation across realities. Nightmarish distortions challenge the stability of the waking world. The ritual, once a potential bridge between realms, now stands as a catalyst for chaos. I must navigate through this upheaval, understanding that the consequences of my choices echo through both Fantasia and the waking world," I pondered, feeling the weight of responsibility for the unfolding cosmic turmoil.

—

Within Fantasia, the eldritch symphony's influence intensified, giving rise to nightmarish embodiments that challenged my very perception of reality. Each manifestation echoed the dissonant notes, distorting the once-stable dream realm.

"As I delve deeper into the heart of Fantasia, nightmarish embodiments confront me at every turn. Distorted reflections of the eldritch symphony's influence, these surreal nightmares test my resolve.

Reality and nightmare intertwine in a dance of chaos, and I press on, determined to confront the source of this cosmic disturbance," I thought, the nightmarish manifestations creating a surreal tapestry of challenge and perseverance.

—

In the waking world, I felt the resonance of Aria's struggle through the echoes. The nightmarish distortions echoed through the realms, a testament to the unseen conductor's influence on both Fantasia and reality.

"The echoes carry Aria's struggle, the nightmarish distortions impacting both realms. The unseen conductor's influence is undeniable, and I grapple with the weight of my role in this cosmic drama. As Aria faces the nightmarish embodiments within Fantasia, I sense the interconnectedness of our destinies, bound by the eldritch symphony that resonates through the fabric of both worlds," I reflected, my connection to Aria's journey deepening as the cosmic forces continued their chaotic dance.

—

As I pressed forward, the nightmarish embodiments became more menacing, each step challenging my very essence. The echoes guided me to the heart of Fantasia, where the unseen conductor awaited, orchestrating the cosmic symphony.

"Confronting these nightmarish embodiments feels like navigating through the twisted corridors of my own fears. The echoes guide me relentlessly, urging me toward the unseen conductor. The surreal nightmares intensify, but I stand firm, determined to unravel the mysteries behind the cosmic disturbance and confront the unseen conductor orchestrating this eldritch symphony," I thought, the challenges only fueling my determination to end the cosmic turmoil.

—

In the waking world, I continued to channel the eldritch symphony, my role as a conduit becoming increasingly apparent. The nightmarish distortions mirrored Aria's struggle within Fantasia, creating a symphony of chaos that tested the boundaries between waking and dreaming.

"As Aria confronts the unseen conductor within Fantasia, I channel the eldritch symphony in the waking world. The nightmarish distortions mirror her struggles, and I realize the profound connection between our actions. The boundaries between waking and dreaming blur as the symphony resonates through both realms. I brace myself for the culmination of this cosmic drama," I pondered, my consciousness becoming a vessel for the cosmic forces that played out in tandem with Aria's journey.

—

The nightmarish embodiments surrounded me, their forms shifting with the discordant notes of the eldritch symphony. As I pressed forward, the symphony intensified its dissonance, echoing through every fiber of my being. I could feel the cosmic forces converging, and with each step, I became a conduit for the unfolding drama.

"The eldritch symphony intensifies, its discordant notes resonating within me. I press on, feeling the weight of my role as a conduit for these cosmic forces. The nightmarish manifestations challenge me, but I stand firm, determined to confront the unseen conductor at the heart of this cosmic disturbance," I thought, my every movement in sync with the ebb and flow of the symphony that bound Fantasia and the waking world.

—

In the waking world, I sensed Aria's struggle through the echoes, the discordant notes reflecting the cosmic upheaval within both realms. My connection to Aria deepened as I channeled the eldritch symphony, becoming aware of the intricate dance between her actions and the unfolding drama.

"As Aria confronts the nightmarish embodiments, the eldritch symphony intensifies its discord. The dissonant notes echo through her being, mirroring the cosmic upheaval that resonates in both Fantasia and reality. Her struggles become intertwined with the symphony, and I feel the weight of our shared destiny," I mused, aware that Aria's every move influenced the cosmic forces that shaped our fates.

—

The surreal nightmares seemed to intensify with the escalating discord of the eldritch symphony. Guided by the echoes, I pressed on, determined to confront the unseen conductor orchestrating this cosmic disturbance. The very fabric of Fantasia quivered with the cosmic forces at play.

"Every step brings me closer to the unseen conductor. The discord of the eldritch symphony reverberates through me, but I press forward, resolute in my quest. The nightmarish manifestations, a reflection of the symphony's dissonance, challenge my every move. Yet, I remain steadfast, driven by the echoes and the cosmic forces that entwine our destinies," I thought, the intensity of the symphony pushing me to the limits of my resolve.

In the waking world, I channeled the eldritch symphony with heightened focus. Aria's struggle against the nightmarish embodiments echoed through the echoes, and I realized her actions' profound impact on the unfolding cosmic drama.

"As Aria confronts the unseen conductor, her every move influences the symphony's discord. The cosmic forces respond to her struggles, and I become more aware of the delicate balance between our actions and the unfolding drama. Aria's influence on the symphony becomes crucial in restoring cosmic equilibrium," I reflected, my role as a conduit gaining newfound significance in the face of Fantasia's unraveling realities.

Chapter 24
Confrontation with the God

I stood at the cosmic threshold, where the boundaries between reality and unreality blurred into a shifting tapestry of eldritch energies. The epicenter of the Dreamlands unfolded before me, a surreal landscape shaped by the disturbed dreams of the sleeping god.

"As I reach the cosmic threshold, the Dreamlands reveal their true nature. The eldritch energies dance around me, the very fabric of reality defined by the god's disturbed dreams. Every step takes me deeper into the heart of the cosmic disturbance, standing on the precipice of an ultimate confrontation," I thought, my senses attuned to the ever-shifting currents of the eldritch tapestry.

—

In the waking world, I felt a resonance with Aria's journey. The echoes carried the essence of her confrontation with the sleeping god, and I sensed the communion between her breath and the eldritch forces that sustained the Dreamlands.

"The cosmic threshold unfolds before Aria, and I, through the echoes, share in the surreal landscape shaped by the god's disturbed dreams. Aria confronts the presence of the sleeping god, and with each breath, she communes with the eldritch forces that intertwine with the very essence of the Dreamlands," I mused, my connection to Aria deepening as the cosmic drama reached its zenith.

—

As I moved closer to the epicenter, the presence of the sleeping god became palpable. Its essence was an amalgamation of disturbed dreams, a force that transcended mortal comprehension. The air itself seemed to vibrate with the god's disturbed dreams, enveloping me in an otherworldly aura.

"Confronting the presence of the sleeping god, I feel the weight of its disturbed dreams. The air around me becomes charged with eldritch energies, and with each step, I draw closer to the heart of the cosmic disturbance. The ultimate confrontation awaits, and I stand ready to face the god that holds Fantasia in the grip of its nightmares," I thought, determination fueling my every movement.

—

In the waking world, I witnessed the unfolding drama through the echoes. Aria's confrontation with the god resonated through the cosmic symphony, and I could sense the magnitude of the cosmic threshold she stood upon.

"As Aria reaches the epicenter, the presence of the sleeping god looms large. The disturbed dreams shape the very fabric of the Dreamlands, and I, through the echoes, bear witness to the cosmic confrontation. Aria's determination becomes a beacon in the eldritch symphony that binds our fates," I reflected, my role as a conduit gaining new dimensions in the face of this celestial showdown.

—

The cosmic threshold plunged me into a nightmarish realm where the god's disturbed dreams materialized as eldritch horrors. These entities, shaped by the deepest recesses of the sleeping deity's subconscious, confronted me with forms that defied mortal understanding.

"As the god's disturbed dreams materialize, I face eldritch horrors embodying the very essence of its nightmares. Their forms are grotesque, twisted manifestations of cosmic struggle. Each step forward brings me face to face with nightmares given life," I thought, my resolve tested by the surreal entities that emerged from the god's subconscious.

—

Through the echoes, I felt the surreal choreography of nightmares unfold. Aria faced eldritch horrors that embodied the cosmic struggle between creation and chaos. The very fabric of the Dreamlands seemed to resonate with the discordant notes of the eldritch symphony.

"The eldritch horrors manifesting from the god's disturbed dreams become a testament to the cosmic struggle. Aria navigates through a surreal dance of nightmares, each entity a guardian of the heart of the cosmic disturbance. The echoes carry the weight of this celestial confrontation," I observed, my connection to Aria deepening as the cosmic drama escalated.

–

The eldritch horrors engaged in a macabre dance, their movements synchronized with the cosmic symphony that echoed through the epicenter of the Dreamlands. Each step I took was contested by these guardians, their movements an intricate part of the eldritch dance that permeated the very air.

"In this surreal dance of nightmares, the eldritch horrors move in harmony with the cosmic symphony. Every step forward challenges me, the guardians weaving a tapestry of cosmic struggle. The echoes guide me through this nightmarish choreography, my every move echoing in the cosmic symphony," I pondered, the ethereal dance becoming a test of both skill and resolve.

—

Through the echoes, I sensed Aria's struggle in the heart of the Dreamlands. The eldritch entities' dance resonated with the cosmic symphony, and I felt the weight of each step she took. The surreal choreography mirrored the ebb and flow of the disturbance that bound both realms.

"Aria navigates through the eldritch dance, her every move resonating in the cosmic symphony. The echoes carry the essence of this ethereal struggle, and I bear witness to the surreal choreography that tests her mettle. The cosmic forces converge, and Aria's journey becomes a pivotal moment in the eldritch symphony," I thought, aware that her actions held the key to restoring balance in Fantasia and the waking world.

The eldritch horrors continued their macabre dance, their movements synchronized with the cosmic symphony. Each step I took was contested by these nightmarish guardians, their forms shifting and contorting in tandem with the dissonant notes that echoed through the Dreamlands.

"As I confront the god's presence and navigate through the eldritch dance, the cosmic symphony intensifies. The guardians' movements are an extension of the disturbance, a surreal choreography that mirrors the cosmic struggle. The echoes guide me, their resonance becoming a beacon in this nightmarish labyrinth," I thought, my determination unwavering despite the chaotic dance that surrounded me.

—

In the waking world, the psychic resonance of Aria's struggle reverberated through my consciousness. The echoes carried the essence of her confrontation with the god, transcending the boundaries between realms. Eldritch echoes whispered in the recesses of my mind, conveying the intensity of Aria's cosmic battle.

"As Aria confronts the god, I feel the reverberations in my waking consciousness. The psychic resonance amplifies the eldritch echoes, creating a bridge between Fantasia and the waking world. Aria's struggle becomes a palpable presence in my mind, and I sense the cosmic forces converging," I observed, the connection between us deepening with each passing moment.

—

The eldritch symphony's dissonant notes echoed through the Dreamlands, and I became aware of Daniel's subconscious becoming a conduit for the psychic echoes. Our connection reached its zenith, the symbiotic link amplifying the cosmic energies that flowed between Fantasia and the waking world.

"As I navigate through the eldritch dance, the echoes guide me, and I sense Daniel's subconscious becoming a conduit for the psychic energies. Our connection deepens, the cosmic dance mirroring the struggles at the heart of the Dreamlands. The boundary between our fates blurs as the cosmic forces weave their intricate tapestry," I pondered, the surreal dance transcending the realms of both dream and waking.

—

The eldritch echoes whispered in the recesses of my mind as Aria confronted the god in the Dreamlands. Our subconscious connection intensified, and I felt the cosmic energies flowing through me, shaping the very fabric of both realms.

"In my waking consciousness, Aria's struggle becomes an integral part of the cosmic dance. Our fates are entwined, and the echoes guide me through the intricate tapestry of the Dreamlands. The boundary between Fantasia and the waking world blurs as the cosmic forces converge in a dance that transcends mortal understanding," I realized, my role in the cosmic drama unfolding with a clarity born from the eldritch echoes.

Chapter 25
Ritual's Culmination

In the waking world, I reached the culmination of the ritual, guided by the intricate pages of "The Everlasting Nightmare." As I followed the steps inscribed within its eldritch verses, a metaphysical convergence unfolded. The very essence of the eldritch symphony resonated within me, and I became a conduit for the cosmic forces that connected Fantasia and the waking world.

"As I complete the ritual, a surge of cosmic energy envelops me. The pages of 'The Everlasting Nightmare' come to life, and I feel the eldritch symphony coursing through my being. I am no longer just an observer; I am a participant in the cosmic drama that unfolds between realms," I mused, my consciousness bridging the gap between the tangible and the ethereal.

—

In the Dreamlands, the symbiotic threads of cosmic energy wove around Daniel, their ethereal glow intertwining with the very fabric of the eldritch symphony. Each step he took in the waking world influenced the ebb and flow of the cosmic energies that pulsed through Fantasia and the Dreamlands alike.

"As Daniel becomes a conduit for the eldritch symphony, I sense the symbiotic threads weaving around him. His actions in the waking world ripple through the cosmic tapestry, resonating with the unearthly music that shapes both realms. The boundaries between our realities blur as the ritual's culmination reaches its zenith," I observed, the cosmic dance now entwining both our destinies.

—

The metaphysical convergence intensified, and I felt the unearthly resonance of the cosmic energies flowing through me. The eldritch symphony responded to the ritual, and my very existence became a bridge, channeling the otherworldly harmonies between Fantasia and the waking world.

"As I embrace the role of a conduit, the unearthly resonance of the cosmic energies deepens. The eldritch symphony acknowledges my connection, and I become a living bridge between realms. The ritual's culmination heralds a new phase in the cosmic drama, and I feel the weight of destiny resting upon my shoulders," I contemplated, aware that my actions were now intertwined with the very fabric of Fantasia's fate.

In the Dreamlands, I sensed the intensifying convergence of realms. The symbiotic threads around Daniel pulsed with cosmic energy, and the eldritch symphony responded to his newfound role as a conduit. The boundaries between Fantasia and the waking world blurred, and the very fabric of our interconnected destinies shimmered with unearthly resonance.

"As Daniel embraces his role, the convergence of realms becomes palpable. The symbiotic threads glow with cosmic energy, and the eldritch symphony acknowledges his presence. Our destinies are no longer separate; they are woven together in a cosmic dance that defies mortal understanding," I realized, my gaze fixed on the shifting tapestry of realities before us.

The unearthly music channeled through me, its ethereal resonance echoing across Fantasia and the waking world. As the cosmic energies flowed through my being, I felt the boundaries between realms blur. The eldritch symphony, once confined to the Dreamlands, became a bridge that transcended the limitations of mortal perception.

"The music courses through me like a cosmic river, connecting Fantasia and the waking world. I sense the pulse of otherworldly harmonies, and the very air shimmers with ethereal resonance. The eldritch symphony, now a part of me, reaches across the realms, intertwining destinies in a dance of cosmic significance," I marveled, my every breath resonating with the surreal music that bound both realms.

—

In the Dreamlands, I felt the reverberations of Daniel's conduit, the cosmic forces responding to the ritual's culmination with a symphony that defied reality itself. The very fabric of Fantasia distorted as the eldritch music coursed through Daniel, altering the essence of cosmic harmony.

"As Daniel becomes the conduit, the reality in Fantasia distorts and shifts. The eldritch symphony, once contained within the Dreamlands, now transcends boundaries. I witness the cosmic forces responding to his presence, creating a symphony that defies the laws of reality. The tapestry of both realms undergoes a metamorphosis, and I navigate through the surreal landscapes, guided by the ever-changing notes of the cosmic symphony," I noted, each step in the Dreamlands mirroring the cosmic dance Daniel orchestrated in the waking world.

—

The ethereal resonance of the eldritch music continued to echo through Fantasia and the waking world. As the conduit for the cosmic symphony, I marveled at the distortion of reality in both realms. The very fabric of existence seemed malleable, responding to the harmony I conducted through the ritual's culmination.

"I am the bridge, the conduit through which the cosmic symphony resonates. Reality warps around me, and I feel the symphony reaching its zenith. The music is no longer confined; it flows across realms, creating a harmonious convergence that defies mortal understanding. Fantasia and the waking world become one in the cosmic dance," I reflected, aware that my actions had set in motion a cosmic ballet that transcended the boundaries of ordinary perception.

—

In the Dreamlands, I navigated through surreal landscapes, guided by the ever-changing notes of the cosmic symphony. The boundaries between realities blurred, and I felt the ethereal resonance of Daniel's conduit reaching across the realms. The distorted reality in Fantasia mirrored the cosmic dance he orchestrated in the waking world.

"As Daniel becomes the conductor, the dance of destiny unfolds. The eldritch symphony transcends the Dreamlands, influencing the very essence of Fantasia. I move through landscapes shaped by the cosmic forces, and each step resonates with the harmonies conducted by Daniel. The destinies of both realms entwine in a surreal ballet, and I continue my journey toward the epicenter of the cosmic disturbance," I declared, the symphony of destiny guiding my every move in the shifting tapestry of realities.

—

In the heart of the Dreamlands, I stood at the cosmic threshold, facing the presence of the sleeping god. As the eldritch symphony echoed through the tapestry of realities, I felt a profound connection with Daniel's performance of the ritual in the waking world. The cosmic confrontation mirrored his actions, creating a dual dance that resonated across Fantasia and the waking world.

"The cosmic dance unfolds in tandem with Daniel's ritual. I confront the god, each movement synchronized with his performance. The eldritch symphony binds us, turning us into conduits that bridge the realms. As I face the embodiment of nightmares, Daniel's actions in the waking world become my guide, and together we shape the destiny of both Fantasia and reality," I proclaimed, the dual cosmic dance unfolding in surreal synchrony.

–

In the waking world, I continued to channel the eldritch symphony through the ritual, feeling the ethereal resonance of Aria's confrontation with the sleeping god. The parallel realities converged, and the cosmic forces resonated in harmony as Aria mirrored my actions in the Dreamlands.

"As Aria confronts the god, I sense the profound connection between our struggles. The eldritch symphony becomes a bridge that spans parallel realities, and the culmination of the ritual intertwines our destinies. Each note I play influences Aria's cosmic dance, and together we shape the resolution of the disturbance that threatens both realms," I acknowledged, aware that our actions in separate realms were intricately connected in the cosmic tapestry.

—

In the Dreamlands, as I confronted the sleeping god, I felt the resonance of Daniel's performance echoing through the cosmic tapestry. The dual cosmic dance unfolded, and the eldritch symphony turned us into conduits that bridged Fantasia and the waking world.

"The confrontation with the god mirrors Daniel's ritual. Our destinies converge as parallel realities become one. The eldritch symphony guides us through the cosmic dance, shaping the very fabric of both realms. In this pivotal moment, the culmination of the ritual becomes the convergence of our destinies, and together we navigate the heart of the disturbance that echoes through Fantasia and reality," I declared, my every movement in the Dreamlands resonating with the harmonies Daniel conducted in the waking world.

—

In the waking world, I continued the ritual, feeling the symbiotic link with Aria intensify. The parallel realities converged, and our actions resonated in harmony as the eldritch symphony guided the cosmic dance. The culmination of the ritual became a pivotal moment, shaping the resolution of the disturbance that threatened both Fantasia and the waking world.

"As Aria confronts the god, I sense the convergence of destinies. Our cosmic dance shapes the very essence of reality, and the eldritch symphony becomes a bridge that binds Fantasia and the waking world. In this moment of profound connection, our actions ripple through the cosmic tapestry, influencing the resolution of the disturbance that spans across parallel realities," I affirmed, realizing that the destinies of Fantasia and the waking world were intricately woven together in this cosmic ballet.

Chapter 26
Unraveling Realities

In the Dreamlands, the eldritch symphony intensified, its dissonant crescendo reaching a point that transcended mortal comprehension. The chaotic resonance of the musical sounds echoed through Fantasia and the waking world, becoming a catalyst for the breakdown of realities.

"The dissonant crescendo reverberates through the very essence of Fantasia and reality. The eldritch musical sounds manipulate the fabric of both realms, pushing them to the brink of cosmic discord. As the vibrations intensify, the boundaries between dreams and waking blur, and the cosmic tapestry that binds our destinies begin to unravel," I declared, feeling the surreal vibrations of the cosmic disturbance shaking the foundations of the Dreamlands.

—

In the waking world, the dissonant notes of the eldritch musical sounds manipulated the fundamental fabric of reality. Fantasia and the waking world experienced a cosmic discord, and I and Aria felt the unsettling vibrations of the cosmic disturbance. The surroundings warped and shifted, responding to the chaotic resonance of the eldritch symphony.

"The dissonant notes permeate both Fantasia and the waking world, causing a cosmic discord that warps the very fabric of reality. The unsettling vibrations shake the foundations of both realms. As the cosmic tapestry unravels, I realize the magnitude of the disturbance we've unleashed. The breakdown of realities becomes imminent, and Aria and I stand at the epicenter of this unraveling cosmic drama," I acknowledged, sensing the profound consequences of our actions.

—

In the Dreamlands, I navigated through shifting landscapes as the dissonant crescendo of the eldritch symphony manipulated the fabric of Fantasia. The boundaries between dreams and waking blurred, and the cosmic discord unfolded with each unsettling note.

"As I move through the Dreamlands, the realities shift around me. The dissonant crescendo of the eldritch symphony warps the very essence of Fantasia, causing landscapes to morph and twist. The breakdown of realities is palpable. I press on, determined to confront the source of this cosmic disturbance," I declared, forging ahead into the surreal landscapes shaped by the chaotic resonance.

In the waking world, I grappled with the unsettling vibrations that echoed through the cosmic tapestry. The eldritch musical sounds intensified, and the breakdown of realities became apparent as the fundamental fabric of Fantasia and the waking world warped and shifted.

"As the unsettling vibrations escalate, I witness the consequences of our actions. The eldritch symphony, once a conduit for balance, now becomes the harbinger of cosmic discord. The breakdown of realities unfolds before me, and I understand that the consequences of our choices reach far beyond what we could have imagined," I admitted, feeling the weight of responsibility for the unraveling cosmic drama.

In the Dreamlands, Fantasia underwent a grotesque transformation, becoming a nightmarish tapestry woven with distorted landscapes and surreal horrors. The eldritch forces reshaped the very foundations of the Dreamlands, warping reality into a grotesque rendition of its former self.

"As I traverse the Dreamlands, the once-beautiful Fantasia now manifests as a nightmarish tapestry. Distorted landscapes and surreal horrors confront me at every turn, a testament to the eldritch symphony's malevolent influence. The foundations of this realm crumble beneath the weight of cosmic disturbance, and the challenge ahead becomes more daunting with each step," I proclaimed, my resolve tested by the ever-changing nightmares confronting me.

—

In the waking world, the nightmarish distortions mirrored the chaos unfolding in Fantasia. The eldritch symphony's influence extended into the mortal realm, causing reality to warp in incomprehensible ways. Cosmic anomalies manifested, blurring the boundaries between dreams and reality.

"As I witness the surreal transformations in the waking world, it becomes evident that the eldritch symphony's influence knows no bounds. Fantasia's nightmarish distortions seep into the mortal realm, manifesting as cosmic anomalies that defy the laws of reality. Aria and I, connected by the threads of destiny, navigate through this kaleidoscope of surreal visions, our struggles intensified by the ever-shifting nature of the cosmic distortions that surround us," I acknowledged, confronting the disorienting challenges presented by the cosmic upheaval.

—

In the Dreamlands, the cosmic anomalies intensified, blurring the boundaries between dreams and reality. Fantasia's nightmarish distortions became an ever-shifting tapestry, challenging my perception and understanding of this once-stable realm.

"The cosmic anomalies persist, blurring the boundaries between dreams and reality. Fantasia's nightmarish distortions weave an ever-shifting tapestry around me, challenging my perception of this realm. Each step is a struggle as I navigate through the surreal visions, determined to confront the source of this cosmic disturbance and restore balance to the Dreamlands," I declared, pressing forward despite the disorienting nature of the ever-shifting realities.

—

In the waking world, the cosmic distortions unfolded, creating a kaleidoscope of surreal visions. Aria and I, connected by the threads of destiny, faced the intensified struggles brought forth by the eldritch symphony's influence.

"The surreal visions persist, and Aria and I navigate through this kaleidoscope of ever-shifting realities. The threads of destiny that bind us become more pronounced as we confront the cosmic distortions that threaten to unravel the very fabric of both realms. Together, we must endure the challenges presented by the eldritch symphony and find a way to restore the delicate balance that has been disrupted," I acknowledged, acknowledging the intertwined fates that propelled us forward in this cosmic drama.

—

In the Dreamlands, the relentless assault of the eldritch symphony took its toll, challenging my ability to discern between reality and nightmare. Fantasia's nightmarish distortions seemed intent on unraveling the very fabric of my sanity.

"As I press forward, the cosmic chaos tests the limits of my sanity. Reality and nightmare entwine in a dissonant dance, making it increasingly difficult to distinguish between the two. Each step is a struggle as the influence of the Eldritch symphony pushes the boundaries of my perception. I grapple to maintain my grasp on the unraveling realities of the Dreamlands," I confessed, the weight of the cosmic disturbance bearing down on me.

—

In the waking world, the cosmic chaos echoed the challenges faced by Aria in the Dreamlands. My sanity frayed as the eldritch symphony manipulated reality itself. However, our symbiotic connection, forged through shared trials, became a source of resilience in the face of the unraveling cosmic tapestry.

"The cosmic chaos threatens to erode the boundaries of reality, challenging my ability to distinguish between what is and what could be. Yet, Aria and I draw upon the symbiotic connection we've forged, each becoming a tether for the other amidst the tumultuous currents of the unraveling cosmic tapestry. Our shared journey becomes the anchor that keeps us grounded as we navigate the chaos that seeks to unravel the essence of both realms," I declared, finding strength in our connection amid the cosmic maelstrom.

–

Fantasia's nightmarish distortions in the Dreamlands intensified, becoming tumultuous currents threatening to sweep me away. The dissonance of the eldritch symphony echoed through the very core of my being.

"The nightmarish distortions become tumultuous currents, threatening to engulf me in their chaotic embrace. The eldritch symphony's dissonance reverberates through the core of my being, and maintaining a foothold in these unraveling realities becomes an arduous task. Yet, the symbiotic resilience forged with Daniel becomes my anchor, a lifeline in the face of the cosmic maelstrom," I declared, pressing forward despite the tumultuous currents that sought to overwhelm me.

—

In the waking world, the echoes of Fantasia's chaos mirrored the challenges faced by Aria. The unraveling realities became tumultuous currents, threatening to drown us in a sea of cosmic discord. Yet, our shared journey provided a lifeline in the face of the relentless assault of the eldritch symphony.

"The tumultuous currents of cosmic discord threaten to drown us in their chaotic embrace. Aria and I, connected by the threads of destiny, draw strength from our shared journey. Our symbiotic resilience becomes a beacon of hope in the unraveling realities as we navigate the cosmic maelstrom together, determined to confront the source of the disturbance that plagues both realms," I affirmed, acknowledging the strength derived from our shared experiences.

Chapter 27
Descent into Madness

The cosmic climax pushed me to the brink of psychic turmoil in the heart of the Dreamlands. The eldritch symphony intensified its dissonant notes, resonating with the unraveling fabric of my sanity. Each step forward was a battle against the encroaching madness, the boundaries between nightmare and reality blurring into a chaotic dance.

"As the cosmic forces reach a crescendo, the eldritch symphony echoes through my mind, threatening to unravel the fabric of my sanity. Madness becomes an alluring abyss, and I teeter on the precipice, grappling with overwhelming sensations that push my mind to the limits of mortal endurance. Each heartbeat echoes with the dissonance of the cosmic climax, and I struggle to maintain my grasp on reality," I confessed, the psychic turmoil threatening to consume me.

—

In the waking world, the shared madness mirrored the cosmic turmoil. Aria and I, connected by the symbiotic threads of destiny, felt the strain of our intertwined fates. The relentless assault of eldritch energies tested the limits of our symbiotic resilience, threatening to unravel the connection that bound us together.

"The symbiotic connection that binds Aria and me faces its sternest test as the shared madness becomes a crucible of cosmic proportions. The strain on our intertwined fates is palpable, and the encroaching madness threatens to erode the very foundation of our connection. We navigate the tumultuous currents of psychic turmoil, our symbiotic resilience wavering under the relentless assault of eldritch energies," I admitted, feeling the strain of the cosmic climax on our shared journey.

—

In the Dreamlands, the chaotic dance of madness unfolded as the eldritch symphony intensified. The dissonant notes echoed through my mind, each reverberation threatening to plunge me into the abyss of insanity. The boundaries between nightmare and reality blurred into a surreal tapestry of cosmic chaos.

"As the cosmic climax propels me further into the chaotic dance of madness, the dissonant notes of the eldritch symphony become a maddening melody that resonates with the deepest recesses of my mind. The boundaries between nightmare and reality blur, and I am entangled in a surreal tapestry of cosmic chaos. The struggle against the encroaching madness becomes a desperate dance. I fight to retain my sanity amidst the cosmic maelstrom," I narrated, the descent into madness becoming an intricate ballet of cosmic proportions.

—

In the waking world, the psychic tempest mirrored the cosmic turmoil in the Dreamlands. Aria and I, connected by destiny's threads, grappled with the overwhelming sensations of madness. The symbiotic strain threatened to unravel the fabric of our shared journey, and the boundaries between waking and dreaming became indistinguishable.

"The psychic tempest mirrors the cosmic turmoil within Aria and me. The overwhelming sensations of madness assail our senses, and the symbiotic strain threatens to unravel the fabric of our shared journey.

The boundaries between waking and dreaming blur into an indistinguishable tapestry of chaos. Together, Aria and I face the descent into madness. This journey challenges the essence of our intertwined destinies," I acknowledged, feeling the strain of the psychic turmoil on our symbiotic connection.

—

As the cosmic climax reached its zenith, eldritch manifestations bridged the realms, their nightmarish forms embodying the very essence of the disturbance threatening to consume Fantasia and the waking world. The boundaries between the Dreamlands and reality blurred as the eldritch entities, once guardians of nightmares, became conduits for chaotic forces beyond mortal comprehension.

"The eldritch manifestations materialize, bridging the realms with their nightmarish forms. They embody the essence of the cosmic disturbance, transcending the boundaries between Fantasia and the waking world. A surreal amalgamation of nightmares takes shape, and I find myself entangled in a cosmic dance with forces that defy mortal understanding," I whispered, witnessing the convergence of nightmares and reality.

—

In the waking world, Fantasia and reality merged in a cosmic amalgamation, the eldritch symphony's influence creating a surreal tapestry where nightmares and reality intertwined. Aria and I navigated through this nightmarish amalgamation, our struggle against the encroaching madness inseparable from the cosmic forces that shaped both realms.

"The cosmic amalgamation unfolds as Fantasia and the waking world merge into a surreal tapestry.

Nightmares and reality intertwine, and I feel the boundaries between realms dissolve. Aria and I navigate this nightmarish landscape, our struggle against the encroaching madness becoming inseparable from the cosmic forces that shape the destinies of both realms. The fabric of reality warps and twists under the influence of the eldritch symphony," I confessed, feeling the surreal tapestry unfold around us.

—

In the Dreamlands, the nightmarish amalgamation unfolded as a chaotic dance of eldritch entities. The once-guardians of nightmares now embodied the cosmic forces that transcended the boundaries between realms. Each movement of the eldritch manifestations echoed the dissonant notes of the symphony, their dance becoming an inseparable part of the encroaching madness.

"The eldritch entities engage in a chaotic dance, their nightmarish forms pulsating with the dissonant notes of the symphony. They bridge the realms, becoming conduits for the chaotic forces that transcend Fantasia and the waking world. The dance intensifies, and I find myself entwined in a cosmic ballet where nightmares and reality become indistinguishable. The struggle against the encroaching madness mirrors the dance that shapes the fate of both realms," I narrated, the chaotic dance becoming a testament to the cosmic forces at play.

—

The surreal tapestry of nightmares and reality unfolded in the waking world as Aria and I navigated through the cosmic amalgamation. The eldritch symphony's influence warped the very fabric of reality, and our struggle against the encroaching madness became inseparable from the cosmic forces that shaped both realms.

"As Fantasia and the waking world merge into a cosmic tapestry, nightmares, and reality intertwine in ways unimaginable. Aria and I navigate through this surreal landscape, our every step contested by the cosmic forces shaping both realms' destinies. The struggle against the encroaching madness becomes an integral part of the cosmic tapestry, each thread woven with the dissonant notes of the eldritch symphony," I admitted, feeling the weight of the surreal tapestry upon our shared journey.

—

The boundary between Fantasia and the waking world blurred further as the cosmic climax unfolded. The ethereal fusion defied conventional understanding, and Aria found herself in a surreal cosmic convergence state. Her physical form and consciousness intertwined with the eldritch symphony that permeated the amalgamated realms.

"The boundary between Fantasia and the waking world blurs even further. I exist in a surreal state of cosmic convergence, my physical form and consciousness intertwining with the eldritch symphony that resonates through the amalgamated realms. The ethereal fusion defies conventional understanding, and I navigate through a reality that transcends the limitations of mortal perception," Aria whispered, feeling the surreal essence of her existence.

–

In the waking world, the boundary between Fantasia and reality experienced a gradual disintegration. The cosmic forces reshaped the fabric of existence, and Daniel was on the verge of madness.

Facing the existential challenge of navigating through a reality that dissolved into the eldritch chaos of the cosmic climax, he grappled with the profound changes that unfolded.

"The boundary between Fantasia and the waking world dissolves even further. Reality undergoes a gradual disintegration, reshaped by the cosmic forces that defy mortal comprehension. I stand on the verge of madness, facing the existential challenge of navigating through a reality that dissolves into the eldritch chaos of the cosmic climax. The very fabric of existence undergoes a transformation, and I am caught in the tumultuous currents of the unraveling realms," Daniel admitted, sensing the profound changes in his surroundings.

—

As Aria and Daniel faced the existential challenge of navigating through the unraveling realms, a sense of cosmic convergence enveloped them. The eldritch symphony resonated through their intertwined existence, and the boundary between Fantasia and the waking world became a shifting tapestry of ethereal energies.

"I navigate through the unraveling realms, and a sense of cosmic convergence envelops me. The eldritch symphony resonates through our intertwined existence, and the boundary between Fantasia and the waking world becomes a shifting tapestry of ethereal energies. Aria and Daniel, caught in the cosmic dance, navigate through the surreal landscape that defies the conventional understanding of reality," Aria described, feeling the cosmic forces guide her through the shifting tapestry.

—

Caught in the tumultuous currents of the unraveling realms, Daniel and Aria struggled to maintain their grasp on sanity. The eldritch chaos intensified, and the ethereal fusion of Fantasia and the waking world blurred the lines between dreams and reality.

"I stand amidst the tumultuous currents of the unraveling realms. The eldritch chaos intensifies, and the ethereal fusion of Fantasia and the waking world blurs the lines between dreams and reality. Interrupted in this cosmic convergence, Aria and I grapple with the profound changes that shape both realms. The struggle to maintain our grasp on sanity becomes an integral part of the cosmic dance that unfolds around us," Daniel admitted, feeling the weight of the shifting tapestry upon their shared journey.

Chapter 28
Echoes of Silence

The eldritch symphony reached its crescendo, and the cosmic forces culminated in a resonant conclusion that echoed through Fantasia and the waking world. The dissonant notes faded into an eerie silence, leaving a lingering sense of otherworldly stillness that transcended the aftermath of the cosmic climax.

"The eldritch symphony reaches its crescendo, the dissonant notes fading into an eerie silence. A resonant conclusion echoes through Fantasia and the waking world, leaving behind a profound stillness that transcends the aftermath of the cosmic climax. The weight of cosmic transformation lingers in the air, and I stand amidst the silence that follows the chaotic symphony," Aria reflected, her senses attuned to the lingering echoes.

—

In the waking world, Daniel felt the harmonious dispersal of the eldritch energies. Their ethereal echoes lingered in the air like a fading melody, and he, too, experienced the profound silence that followed the chaotic symphony. The weight of cosmic transformation pressed upon him, and he navigated through the aftermath, grappling with the echoes of silence.

"The eldritch symphony reaches its conclusion, and the harmonious dispersal of cosmic forces resonates through the waking world. The ethereal echoes linger in the air like a fading melody. A profound silence follows the chaotic symphony, pregnant with the weight of cosmic transformation. I navigate through the aftermath, feeling the echoes of silence shaping the very fabric of reality around me," Daniel acknowledged, sensing the lingering effects of the cosmic climax.

–

As Aria and Daniel stood in the aftermath of the cosmic climax, the lingering echoes of the eldritch symphony painted a surreal landscape. The silence was pregnant with the weight of cosmic transformation, and Aria felt the profound stillness enveloping her.

"I stand in the aftermath, and the lingering echoes of the eldritch symphony paint a surreal landscape around me. The silence is pregnant with the weight of cosmic transformation, and I feel the profound stillness enveloping me. Fantasia and the waking world exist in a state of suspended animation, shaped by the echoes of silence that follow the chaotic symphony," Aria described, her gaze shifting across the altered realities.

–

In the waking world, Daniel shared Aria's perception of the altered realities. The lingering echoes of the eldritch symphony shaped the very fabric of reality, and he marveled at the transformative power that resonated through Fantasia and the waking world.

"I witness the aftermath, and the lingering echoes of the eldritch symphony shape the very fabric of reality around me. The profound stillness is pregnant with the weight of cosmic transformation. Fantasia and the waking world exist in a state of suspended animation, shaped by the echoes of silence that follow the chaotic symphony. I marvel at the transformative power that resonates through both realms," Daniel acknowledged, his awareness attuned to the shifts in the cosmic tapestry.

—

Fantasia and the waking world began to stabilize as the cosmic forces reconciled, the boundaries between dreams and reality finding a fragile equilibrium. Aria stood amidst the altered landscapes, witnessing the subtle shifts as the realms adapted to the aftermath of the eldritch symphony.

"As the cosmic forces reconcile, Fantasia and the waking world stabilize. The boundaries between dreams and reality find a fragile equilibrium. Yet, scars of devastation remain, indelible marks on the landscapes shaped by the cosmic climax. I navigate through the transformed realms, a witness to the aftermath that reshaped the very foundations of our journey," Aria observed, her gaze tracing the remnants of the eldritch disturbance.

—

In the waking world, Daniel marveled at the resilience of reality in both realms. Adapting to the cosmic upheaval, the landscapes showcased a tenacity that defied the inherent fragility of mortal perception. His eyes scanned the transformed landscapes, recognizing the scars of devastation that marked the aftermath of the eldritch symphony.

"Reality showcases its resilience in both realms, adapting to the cosmic upheaval with a tenacity that defies mortal perception's fragility. Fantasia and the waking world stabilize, but scars of devastation remain. I witness the transformed landscapes, my eyes scanning tHe remnants of the eldritch disturbance that reshaped the very foundations of our journey," Daniel acknowledged, a sense of awe in his voice.

—

As Aria and Daniel navigated through the stabilized realms, echoes of transformation resonated in the air. The scars of devastation served as reminders of the cosmic climax that had reshaped the very fabric of their journey. Fantasia and the waking world existed in a delicate balance, their resilience a testament to the enduring spirit of reality.

"I traverse through the stabilized realms, echoes of transformation resonating in the air. The scars of devastation remind us of the cosmic climax that reshaped the fabric of our journey. Fantasia and the waking world exist in a delicate balance, their resilience a testament to the enduring spirit of reality,"

Aria remarked, acknowledging the profound changes that lingered in the aftermath.

—

Daniel shared Aria's perception as they explored the stabilized realms together. The scars of devastation were like chapters etched into the landscapes, each telling a tale of the cosmic disturbance that had challenged the boundaries between dreams and reality. Fantasia and the waking world existed in a fragile equilibrium, the transformative journey leaving an indelible mark on both realms.

"As we traverse through the stabilized realms together, the scars of devastation become chapters etched into the landscapes. Each tells a tale of the cosmic disturbance that challenged the boundaries between dreams and reality. Fantasia and the waking world exist in a fragile equilibrium, the transformative journey leaving an indelible mark on both realms," Daniel articulated, his voice resonating with a profound understanding of the realms' resilience.

–

As Aria and Daniel stood amidst the stabilized realms, forever changed by the cosmic ordeal, they reflected on the transcendent nature of their shared journey. The echoes of silence became a canvas upon which they painted the reflections of their individual metamorphoses, each forever marked by the eldritch symphony.

"The cosmic ordeal has left us forever changed, and as we stand here, reflections intertwining with the echoes of silence, I realize the profound nature of our metamorphosis. Fantasia and the waking world bear witness to the remnants of a cosmic symphony that transcends mortal comprehension," Aria mused, her words echoing in the quiet aftermath.

—

Daniel joined Aria in surveying the aftermath, their fates forever intertwined by the shared journey through the cosmic disturbance. Their symbiotic connection transcended the eldritch symphony that had brought them together. The survey of the aftermath became a testament to the enduring bond forged through the echoes of silence, a bond that echoed in the hushed corridors of Fantasia and the waking world.

"Our fates are forever intertwined, Aria. The cosmic disturbance that brought us together has left an indelible mark on both realms. As we survey the aftermath, the enduring bond we share becomes clear—a bond forged through the echoes of silence, resonating in the hushed corridors of Fantasia and the waking world," Daniel conveyed, a sense of unity in his voice.

—

Aria and Daniel continued to explore the transformed landscapes, each step a testament to the journey that had bound their destinies. The echoes of silence lingered, becoming a tapestry of reflection where the intertwined fates of Aria and Daniel were etched in the fabric of reality.

"The echoes of silence weave a tapestry of reflection, where our intertwined fates are etched into the fabric of reality. Fantasia and the waking world stand as witnesses to the cosmic metamorphosis that has left us forever changed," Aria said, her voice carrying a blend of introspection and awe.

—

Daniel felt the unspoken bond with Aria in the quiet aftermath, a connection that defied the cosmic upheaval. As they surveyed the transformed realms, he realized that the echoes of silence held the essence of their journey. This journey had transcended the boundaries of dreams and nightmares.

"Aria, our journey has been extraordinary. The echoes of silence speak volumes, carrying the essence of our shared odyssey. Fantasia and the waking world may have stabilized. Still, the unspoken bond between us endures, a connection that defies the cosmic upheaval we've witnessed," Daniel expressed, the weight of their shared experiences evident in his words.

Epilogue
Echoes of Transcendence

In the aftermath of the cosmic resolution, lingering echoes resonated through the transformed landscapes. The eldritch energies dispersed, leaving an indelible imprint on the fabric of Fantasia and the waking world. Aria and Daniel navigated through the aftermath, remnants of the eldritch symphony lingering like ghostly whispers.

"As we walk through these transformed realms, I can feel the lingering echoes of the cosmic resolution. The eldritch symphony may have dissipated, but its presence endures in the essence of Fantasia and the waking world," Aria whispered, her senses attuned to the subtle reverberations that touched the very core of reality.

Fantasia and the waking world found a fragile equilibrium, the cosmic forces settling into a celestial serenity that belied the tumultuous events that had transpired. The landscapes, once marred by cosmic chaos, were now bathed in otherworldly tranquility—a testament to the resilience of reality and the cosmic reconciliation that followed.

"The serenity that blankets these realms starkly contrasts the chaos we witnessed. Fantasia and the waking world have found a delicate balance. This celestial calm conceals the cosmic turmoil embedded in their history," Daniel remarked, his gaze scanning the transformed landscapes with awe.

As Aria and Daniel continued their journey through the aftermath, the landscapes painted a transformation picture. The scars of devastation remained, but they were now part of a tapestry that spoke of resilience and cosmic metamorphosis. Aria felt the weight of the cosmic journey, her reflection merging with the transformed surroundings.

"The remnants of the eldritch symphony are like brushstrokes on a canvas of cosmic transformation. Fantasia and the waking world bear the scars, but within them lies a reflection of resilience and the enduring power of reality," Aria reflected, her voice carrying a mix of introspection and wonder.

—

In the celestial serenity that followed the cosmic resolution, Daniel sensed the unwritten future. The echoes of the eldritch symphony had left an indelible mark on both realms. Walking beside Aria, he felt a sense of anticipation—a whisper of possibilities yet to unfold.

"As we move forward, Aria, I can't help but feel the anticipation of the unwritten future. The echoes of the cosmic resolution linger, and within them, I sense the potential for new beginnings and undiscovered realms," Daniel shared, his gaze fixed on the horizon where the celestial serenity met the uncharted territories of their destinies.

II. Aria and Daniel's Fates, Forever Altered by the Eldritch Saga

-

Aria and Daniel stood at the crossroads of their transcendent transformation, the aftermath of the eldritch saga profoundly influencing their beings. The shared journey had left an indelible mark. As Aria felt the cosmic energies resonate within, she realized that the symbiotic connection had evolved into a transcendent bond.

"The eldritch saga has changed us, Daniel. We stand at the crossroads of our transcendent transformation, forever marked by the echoes of the cosmic symphony. The symbiotic connection we forged now transcends the boundaries of mortal existence," Aria mused, her eyes reflecting the cosmic hues that lingered in the air.

–

Aria and Daniel reflected on the cosmic mirror that had shaped their destinies. The silence echoes cast a reflective gaze upon the tapestry of their intertwined fates, revealing the intricate threads woven by the eldritch symphony. Each reflection was a testament to the enduring impact of the cosmic journey on the very essence of their beings.

"As we look into this cosmic mirror, Aria, I see the reflections of our journey. Every twist and turn, every encounter with the eldritch forces—it's all there. The echoes of silence reveal the intricacies of our intertwined fates. This cosmic dance has forever altered the fabric of our existence," Daniel remarked, his gaze fixed on the reflective canvas of their transcendent transformation.

—

The cosmic mirror unveiled the threads of destiny that bound Aria and Daniel. The intricate patterns reflected the trials and triumphs of their journey, each thread a reminder of the cosmic dance they had embraced. Aria sensed the profound connection that transcended the boundaries of time and space, weaving their destinies into a tapestry that defied mortal comprehension.

"These threads of destiny, Daniel, are woven with the cosmic energies that guided us through Fantasia and the waking world. The eldritch forces have left an imprint on our beings, intertwining our fates in a tapestry that extends beyond the limitations of mortal understanding," Aria expressed, her voice carrying the weight of the cosmic revelations.

—

As Aria and Daniel continued to gaze into the cosmic mirror, the enduring impact of the eldritch saga became palpable. The reflections illuminated the resilience forged through shared struggles, the symbiotic connection evolving into a force transcending the cosmic disturbance. Daniel felt a profound sense of gratitude for the transformative journey they had undertaken together.

"The enduring impact of our journey is etched into these reflections. Aria, the eldritch saga, has shaped us in ways we couldn't have imagined. Our connection, forged through cosmic trials, has become a testament to the strength that emerges from the chaos of the unknown," Daniel spoke, his words carrying a resonance that echoed the profound changes they had undergone.

—

As Aria turned the quiescent pages of "The Everlasting Nightmare," she felt a profound sense of closure. The eldritch saga that had unfolded between Fantasia and the waking world was encapsulated within those pages, marking the end of a cosmic journey. Aria and Daniel, having traversed the intricate tapestry of the unknown, closed the book with a reverence for the cosmic forces that had guided their destinies.

"The quiescent pages mark the end, Daniel. Our journey, entwined with the eldritch symphony, has left an indelible mark on these pages. As we close the book, let it be a testament to the cosmic forces that shaped our destinies," Aria spoke, her fingers gently caressing the final pages that held the echoes of their transformative odyssey.

—

The closing pages revealed endless horizons, a narrative that concluded with a sense of cosmic continuity. Aria and Daniel, forever entwined in the echoes of silence, stepped into the endless horizons of their transformed destinies. The resonance of the eldritch symphony echoed in the quiescent pages of

"The Everlasting Nightmare," bridging the tale's finality and the boundless possibilities that stretched before them.

"Aria, these pages may mark the end of a single tale, but the narrative continues in the endless horizons of our transformed destinies. The eldritch symphony's resonance echoes here, connecting the conclusion of our journey with the boundless possibilities that lie ahead," Daniel remarked, his gaze fixed on the pages that held the echoes of their cosmic odyssey.

—

As Aria and Daniel closed "The Everlasting Nightmare," the silence reverberated within the quiescent pages. The cosmic forces that had guided their destinies seemed to linger in the air, bridging the narrative's conclusion and the uncharted realms of their future. Aria felt a sense of fulfillment and anticipation as the eldritch symphony's echoes resonated in their tale's closing moments.

"The echoes of silence, Daniel, linger in these pages. Our journey may have concluded, but the cosmic forces that shaped us continue to whisper in the quiescent spaces between the words. Let us step into the unknown, forever entwined in the echoes of our shared odyssey," Aria spoke, her voice carrying the weight of cosmic revelations.

–

As Aria and Daniel closed the book, they embraced the idea of a cosmic continuum. The quiescent pages held an ending and a beginning—an endless tapestry of possibilities. The eldritch symphony's resonance became a guiding force, transcending the confines of a single narrative. Daniel felt a sense of gratitude for the transformative journey they had undertaken. As they stepped into the endless horizons, he knew their connection would endure in the cosmic continuum.

"Aria, let these pages be a portal to the cosmic continuum. Our journey, guided by the eldritch symphony, is not confined to the boundaries of this tale. It's a perpetual odyssey, and as we step into the endless horizons, let our connection resonate in the eternal echoes of the cosmic forces that bind us," Daniel expressed, his gaze fixed on the quiescent pages that held the culmination of their extraordinary tale.

Afterword

Dear Readers,

    As you close the final pages of "The Everlasting Nightmare," I extend my gratitude for traversing the labyrinthine corridors of cosmic horror and eldritch wonders. Magnum Tenebrosum here, your humble guide through the realms where nightmares and reality dance in macabre unison.

    This literary journey has been a symphony of shadows, a venture into the unknown where the ordinary unravels into the extraordinary. Aria and Daniel's odyssey through the cosmic tapestry was one of revelation, resilience, and the enduring connection that binds them in the echoes of silence.

    As you reflect on the transcendent transformation of these characters, remember that their fates are intertwined with yours. The eldritch symphony's resonance has left its mark not only on Fantasia and the waking world but also on your imagination's very fabric. The cosmic reconciliation, the stabilizing of realities, and the enduring resilience of the characters mirror the human experience in the face of the unknown.

Each nightmare confronted, each dissonant note endured, and each surreal landscape navigated were steps taken into the abyss, challenging perceptions and unveiling the secrets hidden within the cosmic unknown. The quiescent pages of "The Everlasting Nightmare" hold more than tales; they hold reflections of the human psyche when confronted with the unimaginable.

As you step into the endless horizons beyond these pages, let the echoes of silence linger. Embrace the indelible mark left by the eldritch symphony and remember that, like Aria and Daniel, you are forever altered by the cosmic saga.

In the shadows and beyond,

Magnum Tenebrosum

Milton Keynes UK
Ingram Content Group UK Ltd.
UKHW050058180624
444226UK00015B/633

9 798869 126788